Who Goes There?

Molly aimed the flashlight down the straight path in front of her—and stopped short. Her breath caught in her throat.

Climbing down the ladder from the founder's statue was a thin, white-clad figure. The ghost!

The figure on the ladder dropped to the floor and faced them. Molly took a step forward, her thoughts in whirling confusion. "Molly, don't!" Gwen cried, grabbing at her sister's arm.

The ghost glared. Then her finger rose until she was pointing straight at them. "This is your last warning. Get out, or you will regret it!" she cried. "I am the ghost of Mary McPhail!"

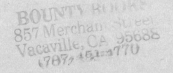

Ghost of a Chance

WELCOME INN

#2 Ghost of a Chance

by E. L. FLOOD

Rainbow Bridge®

Troll Associates

LIBRARY OF CONGRESS CATALOGING-IN-PUBLICATION DATA

Flood, E. L.
  Ghost of a chance / by E. L. Flood.
    p.   cm. — (Welcome Inn; #2)
  Summary: Molly and Josh investigate the mystery surrounding a
ghost and a 100-year-old murder.
  ISBN 0-8167-3428-3 (pbk.)
  [1. Ghosts—Fiction.   2. Mystery aand detective stories.]
I. Title.   II. Series: Flood, E. L. Welcome Inn; #2.
PZ7.F6616Gh   1995
[Fic]—dc20   94-12251

Published by Troll Associates, Inc. Rainbow Bridge is a trademark of Troll Associates.

Printed in the United States of America.

10 9 8 7 6 5 4 3 2 1

For my parents

CHAPTER ONE

"Check this out, Josh!" Molly O'Brien's dark eyes snapped with excitement. She held up a faded photograph in a curling gold-painted cardboard frame and blew a cloud of dust off of it.

Molly's friend Josh Goldberg jerked back. "Hey! Watch it, O'Bri—aah—aah—aah—*tzee! AAH-TZEEE!*" Wiping his watering eyes, he gave Molly an irritable look. "Thanks for blowing dust in my face," he said reproachfully, and sneezed again.

"Oops. Sorry," Molly said.

It was a rainy Wednesday afternoon in November, and the two friends were in the library of the Welcome Inn, the old seaside guest house run by Molly's parents. They were supposed to be looking for books for their social studies reports. But right now they were doing one of the things Molly loved best: simply browsing through the ranks of books that had piled up in the big, shelf-lined room over the years. Many of the books had been there ever since the inn was built, back in the 1860s. A few were even older than the house. And there were *thousands* of books. Molly hadn't even looked at a quarter of them yet, though she'd spent at least a few minutes in the library almost every day since they'd moved in back in June.

After setting the old photograph on the table, Molly wiped it off carefully with the sleeve of her maroon sweatshirt and then handed it to Josh. "Look at this picture. It must be from the real olden days—at least the eighteen hundreds!"

"Whoa!" Josh's face lit up. "Think it's worth something?"

"That's not the point," Molly said. Josh was the coolest kid in the seventh grade, and she was really glad they were friends, but he did spend a lot of time thinking up ways to get rich. "It's from the *olden* days, Josh! Look at the clothes and the girl's hairdo. Just imagine her running around in petticoats and pantaloons—"

"What are pantaloons?"

"Frilly long underwear that girls used to wear. And think of her riding in carriages and stuff like that. It's so cool!"

"It'd be cooler if we could sell the photo for lots

of money," Josh grumbled. But he bent over the table with Molly as she gazed at the picture.

The girl in the photograph looked to be about Molly's age. She wore a lacy white dress and had pale ringlets pulled back from a sweet, thin face. Looking into the girl's huge eyes, Molly had an immediate feeling of kinship. If the girl had lived a hundred years later, they would have been friends—Molly was sure of it.

The girl was seated in a high-backed chair. Behind her stood a tall, thin, stiff-looking man with fair hair parted in the middle and plastered to his head. He wore a dark suit with a funny-looking long jacket that came almost to his knees. He looked worried, Molly thought, observing the faint lines visible between his eyes.

"I wonder who they were," she said softly. She had found the picture pressed inside a huge leather-bound Bible with a metal clasp and a cross embossed on the cover in red. She looked inside the front flap of the big book, but there was no name written on the flyleaf.

"Do you think they lived here?" Josh asked, flicking a lock of brown hair back from his forehead. He had caught Molly's mood, and his voice held the same hushed fascination as her own.

"Could be. Or maybe they were guests here—if the house was an inn back then."

"Molly, Mom says the Hathaways are on their

11

way from the ferry right now," a voice piped up from the doorway. "They'll be here in two minutes, and if you forgot to get Room Four ready for them she's going to kill you." Molly looked up. Her nine-year-old sister, Gwen, stood in the doorway.

"Oh, no!" Molly said. She *had* forgotten. Her alarm grew when she heard a car turn into the long gravel driveway. The Hathaways were here already!

Gwen smirked. She had the same straight dark hair and thin face as Molly, but where Molly's eyes were brown and kind of dreamy, Gwen's were deep blue and always alert.

"I knew you'd forget," she said, coming in and closing the door. "I did it for you."

"You did?" Molly stared at Gwen in shock. "Wow, that was nice of—" Then her eyes narrowed. "Okay, out with it, Gwen. What do you want?"

"To use your room for my slumber party next Friday night," Gwen said promptly. Molly had the greatest room in the house. It was on the third floor at the base of a stubby tower, and it was totally private. Gwen was desperately envious of Molly for having snagged it.

Molly groaned. "Oh, all right," she said. "But if your friend Joanne eats too much again and gets sick in there, I'm going to kill you."

"Don't worry," Gwen said. She gave Josh a smile. "Hi! Are you having dinner with us again?"

"Uh, yeah," Josh said, looking a little embarrassed. He'd had dinner with the O'Briens at least once a week ever since he, Molly, and Gwen had found a pirate treasure chest together back at the beginning of the school year. Molly suspected the prepackaged dinners his harrassed, overworked mother usually made didn't compare too well with Mr. O'Brien's delicious cooking.

"Hey, what's that?" Gwen asked, pointing at the picture. She moved forward and took it out of Molly's hands. "Cool. Who are they?"

"That's what we were trying to figure out," Molly answered.

Frowning, Gwen turned the picture over and ran her fingers along the back of the frame. "Hey, there's something inside here, between the picture and the frame. See? It's all bumpy."

"Give it to me!" Molly said excitedly, snatching the photograph from her sister. She gently pried it out of its frame, careful not to tear the brittle paper.

A slim paper packet fell onto the library table. A faded address was on the front in spidery old-fashioned handwriting. A letter! Molly's fingers tingled as she picked it up, slid a sheet of paper out of the envelope, and unfolded it.

"'My dearest Mary,'" she read aloud. "'By the time you read this I shall most likely be dead.'"

"*Whoa!*" Josh said.

"Eep!" Gwen squeaked, round-eyed.

After a moment's shocked pause, Molly read on with a growing chill.

It is all as I feared. My appeals come to nothing; the court will not hear them anymore. The execution is set for dawn.

It is not for myself that I grieve, but for you, dear child. You must be strong and brave now, and never despair no matter how dark the days may seem. Whatever you may be told, remember always that of this most hideous charge, at least, your father is innocent.

I know I need have no fear for your welfare, as Mrs. Lutz is a most gracious, kind lady and I have no doubt she will make provisions for you. And now I must take my final leave. God bless and keep you, my dear, and be sure that wherever I be, I shall always remain

your loving father,
John McPhail

Everyone was silent for a moment after Molly finished reading. Then Gwen drew in a deep breath. "I feel like crying," she said in a low voice. "Do you think the man who wrote the letter is the man in the picture?"

Molly stared at the photograph. "I think so," she

replied. "They look like father and daughter, don't they?"

"Do you think he was really executed?" Josh asked.

"I don't know." Molly was somber. "I wonder what he did wrong."

"He said he was innocent," Josh pointed out.

Just then a man with a fringe of white hair, a flowing, snowy beard, and eyes the same color as Gwen's stuck his head through the doorway. "Hello there, young ladies," he boomed. "*And* young fellow," he added with a wink at Josh. "Supper's on."

"Hi, Mr. Foster," Josh said.

"Grandpa Lloyd!" Molly cried. If anyone would know about the people in the photograph, it was her grandfather. Lloyd Foster had lived on Blackberry Island all his life, and as far as Molly could tell, he knew everything there was to know about the island, past and present.

"Grandpa," she said anxiously, holding out the photo and the letter to him, "do you know anything about a man named John McPhail?"

Grandpa Lloyd wrinkled his brow. "McPhail," he said. "Seems to me I have heard the name before." He pointed to the man in the photo. "That the fellow?"

"We think so," Molly said.

"And we think he was executed," Gwen added with a shudder.

"Oh, *that* McPhail!" Grandpa Lloyd nodded. "Yes, I've heard his story. Tell you what. Give me a few minutes to eat a bite and get it all straight in my mind, and then I'll tell you about John McPhail."

Molly's parents and her older brother, Andrew, were already seated around the table in the big old-fashioned kitchen when she, Josh, and Gwen came in. "It's about time," Andrew said. "I thought we were going to starve waiting for you."

"Sorry," Molly said, even though she knew Andrew was exaggerating. She didn't feel like fighting with him right now. She slid into her own seat and waited impatiently for her grandfather to eat his soup.

She lasted until he was almost done. Then she burst out with, "Tell us the story, Grandpa!"

Grandpa Lloyd spooned up the last of his clam chowder. Then he wiped his mouth and leaned back in his chair. "Hmm. Let's see, now. . . .

"John McPhail started his career on the wrong side of the law. He was a smuggler in these parts, running rum and such so that folk didn't have to pay the high import and export taxes on it. He had a thriving network here on Blackberry Island. But when he married and had a daughter, he gave that all up and set himself to becoming respectable."

"How come?" demanded Andrew. "I think it'd be cool to be a smuggler."

Molly rolled her eyes. What a dumb thing to say!

"Maybe so," Grandpa said, "but it was a risky profession for a man with a family. And John McPhail loved his wife and daughter very much.

"So he got himself a job as a servant—in fact, as the butler of this very house, back when it was first built."

"Wow!" Gwen said. "So the people in the photo *did* live here."

"Yes, they did. Things went along happily for ten years or so, in spite of the death of Mrs. McPhail from scarlet fever. Little Mary had it, too, and her health was always delicate afterward, but Mrs. Lutz, who built the house, paid for the best doctors for her. Yes, the McPhails must have been happy. John McPhail took to his new life, and I guess he thought he'd put the past behind him."

"Uh-oh," Molly said.

"Uh-oh is right," Grandpa said, nodding. "One day McPhail got a visit from his cousin, Martin Ames. Now, Ames had been McPhail's right-hand man back in the bad old days. He'd tried to go straight, too; even got a job as a bookkeeper for a while. But he was a weak, shiftless fellow and a gambler, they say, and it wasn't long before he was back to running rum.

"Anyway, one day this Ames character came looking for John McPhail. Ames was desperately in need of a thousand dollars to pay off a gambling debt, and he proposed to get that money by smug-

17

gling a huge shipment of rum. But he couldn't do it alone. He needed McPhail to help plan and run the operation.

"I guess McPhail tried to talk Ames out of it. He had no wish to go back to smuggling, not when he had so much to lose. But Ames was his cousin, and Ames said the men he was in debt to would kill him if he didn't pay them off right away. So finally McPhail agreed, and together they made a plan."

"Go on, Mr. Foster," Josh urged as Grandpa Lloyd paused.

"Well, I don't know exactly how it came about, but the law got wind of what the smugglers were up to," Grandpa said, stroking his white beard. "The night the rumrunners' ship came in, it carried a couple of customs agents in disguise. They followed the smugglers into the tunnels—"

"Tunnels?" Molly echoed, startled.

"Yes, didn't I mention that the smugglers had a whole network of tunnels dug under the town? Under a good third of the island, in fact," Grandpa Lloyd said. "Must have taken years to dig 'em all."

Molly and Josh exchanged glances. Tunnels!

"But that night the law finally caught on and stormed the place," Grandpa went on. "There was a great deal of confusion. When it was over and all the smugglers were rounded up, someone noticed that Martin Ames was missing. When the lawmen searched the tunnels, they found out why." He paused and looked around with a serious expression.

"Why?" Gwen asked breathlessly.

"Why?" Grandpa echoed. "Because Ames was lying dead on the cold ground, with John McPhail's knife in his back."

Molly gasped. "McPhail murdered Ames? His own cousin?"

"Well, that's what the jury believed. They agreed McPhail killed Ames after a falling out among thieves," Grandpa Lloyd replied. "But McPhail went to the gallows swearing he was innocent."

"So that's what he was talking about in the letter to his daughter," Molly said. "He told her he didn't do it."

Grandpa nodded. "Mary McPhail never lost faith in her father. She swore he'd been framed, though she didn't know by whom or why. But the shock of his death was too much for the child. She grew weaker and weaker. Only three months later, she herself died." He looked around the table at the rapt faces. "It used to be said her ghost haunted the tunnels, and that folks could hear her faint voice coming from under the ground, crying for justice for her father's name."

"Ohhh . . ." Gwen wailed.

"Wow!" Molly said. A pleasant shiver ran down her spine.

For a moment everyone at the table was quiet, caught in the story's spell. And then, into the silence came slow, deliberate footsteps. They were outside the kitchen door.

And they were coming closer.

CHAPTER TWO

Everyone seemed to freeze. Molly couldn't have moved if she tried. She heard Josh swallow hard. And across the table, Gwen's eyes were two perfect circles.

Then the door swung open.

"Oh, excuse me," said a man's voice. "I just wanted to ask you for a restaurant recommendation. I'm sorry to interrupt."

The tension was shattered. Mrs. O'Brien rose with a laugh. "Excuse *us*, Mr. Hathaway," she said. "We were listening to a ghost story, and I think we got a little carried away. We've got some menus in the parlor. Come with me and I'll show you."

She led Mr. Hathaway out. Andrew snorted. "You were scared, weren't you?" he taunted Molly.

"I saw you jump."

"So did you," Molly retorted.

"Enough, kids," Mr. O'Brien warned.

Josh cleared his throat. "Mr. Foster, are the smugglers' tunnels still there?"

The tunnels! Molly gave Josh an approving look. She'd forgotten about them.

Grandpa Lloyd shrugged. "Well, the mayor ordered the entrance at the smugglers' cove to be walled up after the raid. But, yes, I guess those tunnels are still there to this day."

Molly's heart beat faster. She stood up to clear the table, and Josh jumped up to help. As they carried the dishes to the sink, he whispered, "Are you thinking what I'm thinking, O'Brien?"

Molly nodded with shining eyes. Underground tunnels where smugglers used to hide! Underground tunnels that might even have a ghost in them!

Grandpa Lloyd had said the entrance to the smugglers' cove was sealed. But the tunnels had to come *out* somewhere, didn't they?

"Josh," she murmured. "We've got to find a way into those tunnels."

"I know. But how?" Josh scraped some uneaten food into the garbage. "I mean, we don't even know where to start looking."

"Shh," Molly whispered, jerking her head toward the adults. Even though her parents were pretty great, they still worried if they thought she might be doing something that could possibly— even in the tiniest way—be dangerous. They just didn't have the right attitude about adventures!

As if on cue, Laura O'Brien reentered the kitchen. "Well, I sent the Hathaways off to the Salty Dog. Why don't we have coffee in the parlor, since all the guests are out tonight," she said to Molly's father and grandfather. The adults moved out of the kitchen. Andrew disappeared up the back stairs to his room.

When Molly was alone with Josh and Gwen, she leaned back against the sink. "Okay, here's the plan," she said. "Gwen and I will see if we can find out more about the tunnels from Grandpa Lloyd."

Gwen groaned. "Not another adventure!"

"Gwen!" Molly said severely. Sometimes her younger sister's attitude wasn't too good, either.

"What?" Gwen looked rebellious. "Last time, a mean lady nearly broke my arm and I ended up practically drowning."

Molly folded her arms. "Okay. If you don't want to find the tunnels with Josh and me, that's fine."

"Well, I didn't say that," Gwen muttered. She looked uncertain.

"No, it's fine," Molly said, waving a hand in the air. "You can just stay home."

"Hey!" Gwen protested. She hated to be left out of anything. "Count me in."

"Okay, then." Molly gave a satisfied nod. "As I

was saying, Gwen and I will find out what we can. Josh, meet me tomorrow after school at the bleachers and we'll figure out what to do next."

"Okay. I should go home now," he said. "I have some stuff to do."

Molly and Gwen walked him to the front door. As they passed the parlor, Josh said, "I'd better say good night to your folks." Molly opened the parlor door.

Inside, the adults were all standing around the TV, watching intently.

"Shh!" Mrs. O'Brien raised a hand as Molly started to speak. "In a minute."

"She was last seen yesterday on her way to school, wearing a navy-blue jacket," the newscaster was saying. In a corner of the screen was a grainy black-and-white photo of a little girl with tousled hair and a sulky expression. "Though they have received no ransom demands to date, police fear that Carrie, who is the granddaughter of Blackberry Island millionaire Edward Hewitt, may have been kidnapped."

Kidnapped! Molly's eyes widened.

"She is eleven years old, slim, with wavy blond hair and blue eyes. Anyone with any information on her whereabouts is asked to call the number on your screen. In other news—"

Mrs. O'Brien leaned down and snapped off the TV. "That poor child! Kidnapped!" she said. "I hope it isn't true!"

"Were they talking about Carrie Hewitt?" Josh asked. "The same Carrie Hewitt who used to live here on the island?"

Mr. O'Brien nodded.

"Do you know her?" Molly asked.

"Our mothers were friends. We used to play together when we were little," Josh said. He looked a little shaken. "But our families lost touch when the Hewitts moved to Connecticut a few years ago."

"I remember that," Grandpa Lloyd said. "Word was that that mean old buzzard Ed Hewitt fought so much with his daughter-in-law that he drove the family away."

"Really?" Molly said, wanting to hear more.

"Dad!" Mrs. O'Brien eyed Grandpa Lloyd reproachfully. "That's just gossip. I'm sure they left because one of them got a good job on the mainland. Just like I did."

"But you came back, didn't you?" Grandpa Lloyd retorted. His face softened. "Ed's son, Jim, never got the chance to come back, poor fellow. He was killed in a car accident two years ago. I guess Elsa's been raising Carrie on her own since then." He sighed. "Lots of trouble in that family."

Mr. O'Brien cleared his throat. "Let's just hope Carrie gets back to her mother safely." He looked at Josh. "I'll drive you home, Josh. Wouldn't want your mom to worry."

❖ ❖ ❖

25

"Rats! This is a dead end," Molly said. She kicked at a metal fence post at the edge of the ferry dock, then hopped on one foot as pain shot through her big toe. "Ow!"

It was Thursday afternoon after school, and it was a drizzly but warm fall day. Molly, Gwen, and Josh were looking for entrances to the old smugglers' tunnels. So far, they were having no luck at all.

"Why did your grandfather think there might be an entrance here, anyway?" Josh asked.

"This is where smugglers' cove was," Molly explained. "Grandpa said that before they dredged out the harbor and built the ferry wharf, this place was all a big tidal swamp. The smugglers used to land goods here because it was so isolated. They had a tunnel right at the dock so they could carry stuff to and from the boats without being seen."

"I guess that makes sense," Josh allowed. He gazed around at the bustling wharf. "But if there ever was an entrance here, it got cemented over a long time ago. And we can't dig through cement."

Molly shook drops of water from the hood of her raincoat. "Okay, let's try somewhere else. How about the place where Martin Ames used to live? He was one of the main smugglers. Doesn't it seem likely that he might have had an entrance somewhere around his house?"

"Ugh," Gwen said. "Didn't Grandpa say Martin

Ames's house is now Mr. Cole's antique store? He's mean. I think he hates kids. He always looks at me funny when I go in there with Mom."

"We're not going in," Molly pointed out. "We can't go poking around inside his store, searching for trapdoors and stuff. We just have to hope there's a way into the tunnels from the outside."

Josh nodded. "Let's hurry," he said. Looking embarrassed, he added, "I, uh, I have to get home soon."

"Is your mom all worried because of what happened to Carrie Hewitt?" Molly guessed.

Josh nodded. "The story was all over the news this morning. Mom really freaked. She wanted me to come straight home after school and not go out at all. Can you believe it?"

"Our mom was the same way," Molly admitted. "I hope Carrie Hewitt gets rescued soon. It's going to be even harder to find the tunnels if our parents never let us out of the house!"

The streetlights came on as the three of them trudged up the steep hill from the ferry dock to High Street, then turned left onto Oak. Mr. Cole's antique shop was a tall, narrow house in the old section of town. The building had a pinched, tight look about it that reminded Molly of its owner.

"Let's look around the back," she suggested.

Molly led the way through Mr. Cole's side yard and around to the back of the house. There wasn't much there—just a small brick patio and some trash cans. The only door led to Mr. Cole's utility room, where he kept antiques that needed to be restored.

"Doesn't look like we're going to find any tunnels here," Josh said.

"Good. Let's go home before Mr. Cole sees us," Gwen said.

Just then there was a sharp rapping on the window of the utility room. Molly jumped.

A second later the door flew open and Mr. Cole stood on the top step. "What are you kids doing back here?" he demanded angrily.

"Hi, Mr. Cole. We were just, um . . . looking for something," Molly stammered. *Oh, good answer!* she told herself. *Really smooth!*

"What could you possibly be looking for in my yard?" he asked irritably. With his round face and his quivering, red-tipped nose, Mr. Cole was like a giant rabbit, Molly thought. A fussy, irritable rabbit.

"What are you smirking at?" he called.

"Uh—nothing," Molly said hastily. She gulped back a giggle and beckoned to the others. "Sorry we disturbed you, Mr. Cole."

He didn't move from the top step. "Go on, get out of here before I call your parents!"

"We're going, we're going," Josh muttered, stalking through the side yard. He turned to Molly and rolled his eyes. "He acts like we were breaking in or something."

"I told you he didn't like kids," Gwen said. "Can we go home now?"

Molly glanced at the fading light in the sky. "I guess we'd better."

"So what do you think we should do tomorrow?" Josh asked. "I mean, poking around in people's yards doesn't seem like such a good way to find these tunnels."

"Do *you* have a better idea?" Molly snapped.

"Chill, O'Brien," Josh said. "I didn't mean it that way. I just think maybe we should try to come up with some other plans, okay?"

"Okay," Molly muttered. "See you later."

She and Gwen hurried up Oak to Main Street, past Founder's Green with its tall brass statue of Jan van Huyten, the first settler on Blackberry Island. As she walked, Molly admitted to herself that Josh was right. They *weren't* going to get very far by poking around in people's yards. There had to be a more logical way to find the tunnels.

The girls went past the gas station and the tire store. Then they were out of town. Main Street changed into Route 38, the road that ringed Blackberry Island. Welcome Inn sat atop a small hill a quarter of a mile ahead on the left. Its crooked tower and jumbled roof peaks made it look almost like a haunted house from a movie.

Of course, Molly's thoughts ran on gloomily, it was possible that all the tunnel entrances really had been sealed off. In that case, they were never going to find a way in.

Her lips tightened. "No! There has to be a way!" she said aloud.

"What?" asked Gwen.

"Nothing," Molly said. Suddenly she was tired of thinking about the tunnels. Settling the straps of her backpack more firmly on her shoulders, she looked at her younger sister. "Come on, I'll race you home. Last one there's a rotten egg!"

On Friday, Molly came home from school feeling happy. First of all, they'd gotten out of school unexpectedly early because the heaters went haywire. Second, she'd gotten good grades on both a French test and a math test. But the third thing was the best: Ann Chiu had invited her to a sleepover the following weekend.

When Molly had first come to Blackberry Island Middle School, she hadn't had any friends, and Ann hadn't been all that interested in getting to know her. Ann was friends with Charlotte Anderson, who didn't like Molly and was always looking for mean tricks to play on her.

But after Molly and Josh had found the pirate treasure, Ann had started paying attention to Molly, even though it made Charlotte really mad. Now they ate lunch together a lot and Ann was helping Molly get to know some of her friends. But this was the first time any of the girls had invited Molly over. It was a big step!

When Molly got home, only her father was there, engrossed in the latest issue of *Coleoptera Journal.* Mr. O'Brien studied bugs in his spare time. Molly stuck her head into the study. He looked startled to see her.

"Is it four o'clock already?" he asked.

"School let out early," Molly explained.

Mr. O'Brien smiled. "Lucky you. Want to see a beautiful picture of a dung beetle in molt?" he added hopefully.

"Maybe later, Dad," Molly said, quickly closing the door. Michael O'Brien usually didn't talk much, but once he got started on bugs, there was no stopping him.

Grabbing an apple from the kitchen, Molly headed for the library. She wanted to ponder how to find an entrance to the smugglers' tunnels, and the library was the place where she thought best.

Molly wandered around the room, idly running her fingers over the spines of the old books as she thought. Would the old newspapers from the time of the big raid tell anything about where the other entrances were? she wondered.

She bit into her apple and savored the crisp sweetness. Maybe she should go to the town library tomorrow and see if they had newspapers going back that far. It was kind of neat to think of reading through all those old accounts, searching for one tiny tidbit of information. She'd never done anything like it before. She felt almost like a real detective.

Molly frowned as she noticed a black book that was placed upside down on a shelf above her head. It was just out of her reach. *I bet Andrew was the one who put it back wrong,* she thought as she went to fetch a stool.

After setting the stool in front of the shelf, Molly stood on the seat and reached for the upside-down book. For a second it didn't budge.

Then it tipped out and down, pivoting on the shelf as if it were hinged at the bottom. Molly gave a squeak of alarm and jumped backward off the chair. The whole bookshelf was moving toward her!

The shelf swung smoothly out from the wall, knocking the stool over with a clatter. Molly's heart pounded as she peered cautiously into the blackness behind the shelf. She knew at once what she had found.

"A secret passage!" she whispered in awe.

But where did it go? Molly could make out a narrow flight of stone steps leading down into the dark. She had to see where they led. Taking a deep breath, she started down.

There were eleven steps. At the bottom was a wooden door. Molly reached for the old-fashioned latch, sure the door would be locked.

But it wasn't. The latch lifted slowly under her hand with a protesting squeak. Then the door swung open. Once more Molly was faced with blackness, only this time it was solid, inky. A current of cold, dank air whispered past her face. She stuck her head through the doorway. "Hello?" she said, trying to keep her voice steady.

"Ello? Lo?" came a faint echo a moment later.

Molly stepped back, closed the wooden door, and leaned against it. Her heart was beating wildly. "I've got to get Josh and Gwen," she muttered. "They're never going to believe it."

The truth had just hit Molly in a flash. The secret passage in the library of Welcome Inn led right into the old smugglers' tunnels!

CHAPTER THREE

Molly bounded up the eleven steps to the library in a fever of excitement. She had to call Josh right away!

As she reached the library door, though, the murmur of voices outside stopped her in her tracks.

"Of course we can give you a room," Mr. O'Brien was saying. "It's our pleasure."

"I'm sorry I didn't call ahead to reserve," a woman's voice said. She sounded tired and anxious. "I've just had so much on my mind. . . ."

"Don't worry about it," Mr. O'Brien said in a reassuring voice. "At this time of year, there are so few tourists on the island that a reservation isn't necessary." He gave a rueful chuckle. "To tell the truth, reservations are hardly ever necessary here at

Welcome Inn. Since we opened the place in July, we haven't been full yet.

"Now, if you'd care to wait in the parlor, I'll see about getting a room ready for you."

"Thanks," the woman said. Molly heard the door open across the wide hall.

"Molly?" her father's voice called. "Molly!"

The secret passage! Molly darted back to the bookshelf that still stood ajar, jumped up like a slam-dunker, and flipped the upside-down book back into position.

The shelf swung shut. There was the faintest of clicks as it settled into place, but that was all. As the library door opened, Molly tried to control her breathing and look innocent.

"Molly?" Her father seemed mildly puzzled. "Didn't you hear me calling you?"

"I . . . I guess I wasn't paying attention," Molly said. It wasn't exactly the truth, but you couldn't really call it a lie, either.

Mr. O'Brien shrugged. "Listen, we have an unexpected guest. Mrs. Hewitt is going to stay with us for a couple of days."

Molly's eyes widened. "Mrs. Hewitt?" she repeated. "You mean Carrie Hewitt's mother? What's she doing here?"

Mr. O'Brien lowered his voice. "I think she's come to try to patch things up with her father-in-law," he said. "If they do get a ransom note for

Carrie, she wants to be sure he's willing to pay."

"You mean he might not be?" Molly asked, shocked.

"I'm sure he is," Mr. O'Brien answered. But he seemed troubled. "At any rate, that's none of our business. All we can do is give her a nice room and make her stay as pleasant as possible."

"I'll go get Room One ready," Molly offered.

Her father smiled absently. "Thanks."

On her way to the back stairs, Molly couldn't resist peeking through the spy hole in the wall that separated the dining room and the front parlor. The spy hole was actually a gap where the chimney of the parlor's wood stove didn't quite meet the wall. There was a pretty good view of the parlor through it. Molly and Gwen often used it to scope out new guests.

Mrs. Hewitt was sitting on the love seat in front of the windows. Her hands were in her lap and she was staring down at them. At first, all Molly could see was a bunch of curly dark hair, pulled into a loose bun. Then Mrs. Hewitt looked up.

Her face was lined with exhaustion and worry, and her brown eyes were full of tears. As Molly watched, they spilled down her cheeks. She didn't try to wipe them away. She simply sat there, not moving, not speaking, not even sniffling. Just crying those silent tears.

Tears rose in Molly's own eyes. Suddenly she felt

awful for spying. She backed away from the gap by the chimney and hurried toward the stairs.

"How come all the exciting stuff happens to you?" Josh grumbled. "First you find a secret passage in your own house, and then the mother of a missing kid comes to stay with you."

"I wouldn't call that part exciting," Molly said. She thought of the sad, lost look on Mrs. Hewitt's face. "I feel sorry for her."

"Shh," Gwen said. "She's coming out."

It was later that afternoon, and Molly, Gwen, and Josh were in the kitchen, waiting impatiently for a chance to get into the library and explore the secret passage. The problem was that Mrs. Hewitt had been in the library ever since Josh arrived. She was looking for something to read.

Molly peeked through the doorway and saw Mrs. Hewitt start up the stairs with a book in her hand. "Come on," she whispered. Raising her voice, she called, "Dad, we're going outside."

"Okay," Mr. O'Brien called from his study. "Don't go far, and be sure to be home in time for supper. Josh, want to stay and eat with us?"

"Sure, thanks, Mr. O'Brien," Josh replied, grinning.

The three kids tramped noisily out the front door, then sneaked back in. Molly shut it with a bang and jerked her head toward the library.

They tiptoed noiselessly inside and Molly eased

the door closed. Her heart was starting to pound again. "Over here," she whispered, heading for the section of bookshelf that swung out.

This time, when she climbed onto the stool and pulled down the black book, she was prepared for what came next. As the shelf swung toward her, she leaped lightly off the stool and whisked it out of the way. Behind her, Josh and Gwen gasped in astonishment. Molly felt an excited grin stretch across her face from ear to ear.

She looked at the other two. "Ready?" she whispered.

Josh nodded, his green eyes glowing. Gwen simply stared with her mouth open.

"Josh, you go first," Molly ordered. "Did you bring your flashlight like I told you?"

"Got it." Josh held up a slim black flashlight. A piece of masking tape marked "GOLDBERG" was wrapped around one end. Switching it on, he started down the steps.

"You next, Gwen," Molly told her sister.

Gwen gulped and followed Josh. Molly whisked through the doorway behind Gwen and tugged on the small knob that stuck out from the back of the shelf. The secret door slowly swung closed.

At the bottom of the stairs, Gwen and Josh had the wooden door open and were craning their necks to peer into the dark passage that lay beyond. "Go on," Molly urged.

Josh stepped through the doorway, then Gwen, then Molly, her pulse racing with feverish excitement. And then they were all standing in the smugglers' tunnel.

It was pitch black. Josh beamed his flashlight in a wide arc around them. The yellow cone of light moved over rough earth walls and a low ceiling from which an occasional tree root dangled. Beyond the range of the light, the tunnel disappeared into blackness in both directions.

"Wow," Gwen said in awed tones.

"Cool," Josh added.

Molly said nothing, but a thrill ran down her spine.

"Which way should we go?" Gwen asked.

"Let's go right," Molly said, after thinking about it for a while. "Toward town. That's where all the interesting stuff should be."

"What do you think is at the end of the left fork?" Josh asked.

Molly shrugged. "There's not much that way except a few old houses. Maybe the smugglers had another landing place on one of the oceanside beaches, though."

They set off, all three of them walking side by side down the wide passage. There was a raw, earthy smell, but the air was fresher than Molly had expected. It was chilly and damp, though. She was glad they'd all worn jackets.

The tunnel sloped steadily down for a while, then leveled out. As far as Molly could see into the blackness ahead, it ran straight as an arrow, with no side tunnels branching off.

"There's one thing I don't get," Josh said. "Why is there an entrance to the tunnels from Welcome Inn?"

Molly glanced at him in surprise. "Well, it makes sense, doesn't it? John McPhail lived there, and he was the head smuggler, right?"

"Yeah, but Grandpa Lloyd said John McPhail gave up smuggling to become a butler," Gwen objected. "And he couldn't have moved into the inn *before* he became Mrs. Lutz's butler. That wouldn't make any sense."

"Oh," Molly said, taken aback. She hadn't thought of that.

"Well," she said after a moment, "maybe he didn't really give up smuggling." She felt a pang of disappointment as she said this. She'd liked the idea of the noble smuggler, reforming out of love for his family. But maybe McPhail hadn't really been that kind of person.

"It still seems weird," Josh muttered.

"Hey, what's that?" Gwen said suddenly. "There's something up ahead on the left!"

Josh hurried forward and aimed the light where Gwen was pointing. A dark hole yawned in the earthen wall of the tunnel—a side branch!

Molly and Josh exchanged glances.
take it," Josh said.

Molly nodded. "Let's go!"

The branch was much narrower than the main tunnel, so they had to walk single file. Gwen insisted on going in front. "After all, it's my branch," she said. "I found it."

"It isn't *yours*. We would have found it a second later," Molly grumbled. "It would have been hard to miss." But she let Gwen go first.

Once again, the ground sloped down under their feet. Then the tunnel branched again. Soon a fishy, salty tang hung in the air—the smell of the sea. "We must be getting near the beach," Josh said.

All of a sudden Gwen shrieked and dropped the flashlight she'd been holding. A second later her fingers were digging into Molly's arm. The light rolled across the floor and went out.

"What! What happened?" Molly cried.

"Something ran across my foot!" Gwen wailed.

"Oh, for Pete's sake," Josh muttered. There were some fumbling noises in the dark, and then the light came back on. He shone it in Gwen's face. "It was probably just a rat," he told her matter-of-factly.

"A *rat*?" Gwen's voice rose to a shriek. "*A rat*? I want to go back!"

"Maybe we should," Molly said. "It's getting late, and we don't want Mom and Dad to start wondering where we are."

Josh peered at his watch. "It's not even five o'clock yet!" he said, his voice exasperated. Then his eyes narrowed as he looked at Molly. "Hey. Are you scared of rats, too?"

"No!" Molly insisted.

Josh shook his head. "I should have known. Women," he muttered in disgust.

"I am not scared of rats," Molly declared. She grabbed the flashlight from Josh. "Give me that. I'll go first!"

"But I want to go back," Gwen moaned.

"Be quiet," Molly told her, and stomped off down the tunnel.

Soon the soil under her feet turned sandy and damp. The smell of saltwater and dead fish got even stronger, and Molly thought uneasily that rats were probably attracted to it. Not that she was scared of any dumb rats, but still . . . She was relieved when she found another branch in the tunnel, this one on the right side.

This branch went uphill, and it was wide enough for two people to walk side by side. Josh caught up with Molly while Gwen straggled behind, muttering rebelliously to herself.

"Hey, stop for a second," Josh said suddenly. "I thought I saw a light. Look, there by the fork in the tunnel."

Josh was right. A weak, thin shaft of light slanted down from the ceiling ahead of them. By its glow

they saw a slender iron ladder leading up
hole in the earthen ceiling. When Molly aime
flashlight up, all she could see was a sort of lump,
odd-shaped black tunnel.

She stared in wonder. "Where do you think it goes?"

"Let's check it out. O'Brien, you can go first," Josh said generously.

"Thanks," Molly said, not at all sure whether she really wanted to. Still, she wasn't going to admit that to Josh. Stepping onto the rungs of the ladder, she climbed swiftly up toward the light.

At the top of the ladder she stopped. "Everything okay up there?" Josh called.

Molly didn't answer. She was too busy trying to figure out what she was seeing.

It was part of the town, that she knew. She could see houses, trees, and a sliver of the sunset through two small holes in the wall in front of her. The wall seemed to be made of something smooth and hard, not earth. She rapped her knuckles on it and it gave out a hollow note. Metal!

At the clang, there was a sudden flurry as a flock of pigeons started up in fright. A gray feather drifted past Molly's startled gaze.

Suddenly she gave a laugh of sheer delight as she realized where she was. "We're right under Founder's Green!" she called down to Josh and Gwen. "I can see the bandstand. You guys aren't going to believe this. I think I'm looking through the eyes in Jan van Huyten's statue!"

"Are you serious?" Josh exclaimed. "That's so cool! Hey, O'Brien, come down from there. I want to have a look, too."

"In a min—" Molly's words were cut off when Gwen let out another shriek. Swiftly Molly dropped to the floor of the tunnel.

"Did a rat run across your foot again, Gwen?" she asked.

"No," Gwen said. "It was a person!"

Josh frowned. "A person ran across your foot?"

"No! I *saw* a person. In there." Gwen pointed toward the fork of the tunnel. "But she disappeared."

"Gwen, that's impossible," Molly said.

"I saw her!" Gwen insisted.

"What did she look like?" Molly asked.

Gwen shrugged. "Like a kid. She was about as tall as you, I guess. Skinny. She had blond hair. And she was wearing white."

Molly felt cold. "White?" she echoed.

"I think so," Gwen said. "It was kind of dirty, though. . . ." Her voice trailed off as she realized what Molly was asking. She gulped.

"O'Brien," Josh said. "You don't think—"

Molly nodded solemnly. "I do think," she said. "It fits."

"I guess so," Josh agreed.

Molly put her hands on her sister's shoulders. "Gwen," she said, "I think you just saw the ghost of Mary McPhail."

CHAPTER FOUR

"I was hoping you weren't going to say that," Gwen said in a small voice.

"Don't be scared," Molly told her. "If it is Mary McPhail, she's a *good* ghost."

"That makes me feel a lot better," Gwen said. "Can we go home now?"

"Of course not!" Molly was shocked. "We have to find the ghost! If she's still hanging around down here, obviously she's waiting for someone to prove her father wasn't a murderer. We need to tell her we're going to work on it, poor thing. Now, show us exactly where you saw her."

"Wait a minute! Slow down," Josh said. "I'm with Gwen. We should go now."

Molly faced him in disbelief. "What? Are you

scared, too? I can't believe it."

"I'm not scared. But we shouldn't just jump right in. We don't know for sure that she is a good ghost," Josh said. He held up a hand as Molly started to interrupt. "We *don't* even know for sure that John McPhail was innocent."

"Why else would Mary's ghost be here?" Molly sputtered. She was starting to lose her temper.

"I don't know. Maybe she's mad that they hanged him. Maybe she wants . . . revenge." Josh said the last word in low, spooky tones. Then he went on in a normal voice. "Anyway, if we don't go back now, your parents will wonder where we are."

"Yeah!" Gwen agreed.

"Oh, all right," Molly muttered. "But you're wrong, Josh." Under her breath, she added, "And I think you're scared."

Josh rolled his eyes. "Come on—this way," he grumbled.

He led the way, hurrying along the rough-packed floor. "Left here," he said, veering into a dark opening in the tunnel wall. A second later he yelped, "Hey! The way is blocked!"

"Oh, no!" Molly ran forward, then stopped short as she stared at a tumbled mound of earth and rocks that blocked the tunnel.

"The ceiling must have caved in," Gwen said in a forlorn voice. "We're trapped!"

"Oh, brother," Josh said.

Panic rose in Molly, but she pushed it down. She needed to think. "Wait," she said.

Gazing at the mound that blocked the way, she noticed that it was packed down hard. Water had collected in tiny hollows on its sides.

"Hey, you guys," she said slowly, "this roof looks like it caved in a while ago. And we'd have heard something if it happened while we were down here. I think we took a wrong turn, that's all."

"So we're not trapped, we're just hopelessly lost," Gwen said. "Great!"

"Calm down," Josh advised her. "We'll find the way out. I have a good sense of direction."

"Then how'd we get lost in the first place?" Gwen muttered. But she followed Josh and Molly as they backtracked.

They trekked on for several minutes, veering into branch after branch of the web of tunnels. "Josh," Molly called uneasily, "I don't remember making this many turns."

"I know where I'm going," he called back.

"*Whoooooooo* . . . " A strange, hollow moan suddenly filled the air.

"Eeeek!" Gwen screamed. "It's the ghost! She's after us!"

Molly shivered. Could it be?

"It's not the ghost," Josh said. "It's the wind."

Wind? Underground? Molly wondered. But she didn't say it out loud. And she noticed that in spite of his words, Josh started moving faster.

All three of them sighed with relief when, suddenly, they popped out into what Molly thought of as the main tunnel—the one where they could all walk side by side.

"This way," Josh said in a firm voice, and turned right.

Molly caught up to Gwen and took her sister's hand. "We're almost there," she said quietly.

A few minutes later they were filing through the wooden door that led to the stone steps. Molly climbed the flight noiselessly and listened at the top for any sound from the library. Hearing nothing, she turned the little knob on the back of the secret panel.

The panel swung out silently. She exhaled the breath she'd been holding and stepped into the library.

Josh came in last, and Molly directed him to shut the secret panel. Then she took a seat at the long wooden table and folded her hands. "Okay. Let's decide what we're going to do about the ghost in the tunnels."

"Let's not do anything," Gwen suggested.

Molly ignored that and looked at Josh. "I want to help Mary McPhail. I think we ought to at least read up on what happened."

He shrugged. "I'm up for it. It'd be cool if we solved a hundred-year-old mystery. I just think we shouldn't jump to any conclusions about whether

Mary McPhail is a good ghost or not. But I want to check out the tunnels, no matter what."

"Good. So it's settled," Molly said happily.

"I guess you don't care what I think," Gwen said.

"Come on, Gwen, it'll be fun!" Molly reassured her, seeing the hurt look on her sister's face.

"Fun, ha!" Gwen retorted. "All right, I'll help. But, Molly, if that ghost slimes me or anything like that, I'm telling!"

On Saturday morning, Molly and Josh planned to go to the public library to look up old newspaper articles on the trial of John McPhail. When Molly finished dressing, she went down to the kitchen, where Gwen was eating a bowl of cereal.

"Hi," Molly said, and headed for the refrigerator. She was gulping orange juice from the container when her mother bustled through the swinging door from the dining room. Molly started guiltily and replaced the container in the refrigerator. Mrs. O'Brien hated it when people drank from the container.

But this time Laura O'Brien didn't even seem to notice. She dumped an armload of newspapers on the kitchen table and shook her head, setting her cap of reddish-brown hair swinging.

"Sometimes I wonder where your father's head is," she said to the girls. "I can't believe he left all these papers lying in the dining room where Mrs.

Hewitt might find them. The last thing she needs is to see her troubles raked over in one of these rags."

"What do they say?" Molly asked, picking up one of the papers curiously.

WILL HE OR WON'T HE? screamed the headline. Underneath, in smaller type, Molly read, "Miserly millionaire cut family off without a penny. Will he pay the ransom now?"

"Listen to this." Gwen picked up another of the papers. "'More Heartbreak for Hewitt—Psychic Sees Ancient Curse!'" Her eyes moved down the page. "Wow. First the family had this humongous quarrel, and Mr. Hewitt stopped speaking to everyone else, then his only son was killed in a car crash, and now his only grandchild has been kidnapped. The psychic thinks the family is cursed." Suddenly Gwen let out a gasp. "And she thinks Carrie was taken by aliens! That's why there hasn't been any ransom note."

Mrs. O'Brien groaned. "Now do you two understand why I didn't think Mrs. Hewitt would want to see these stories?" she asked.

"I guess the psychic thing is kind of silly," Gwen said. "But the stories do make you wonder."

"Yeah," Molly agreed. "Is old Mr. Hewitt really as mean as he sounds?"

Mrs. O'Brien heaved a big sigh. "How about if we just drop the subject?"

Molly pulled off her jacket from its peg by the

door. "Don't tell me you're getting ready to go without me nagging you," Mrs. O'Brien said.

"Go where?" Molly asked, puzzled.

Mrs. O'Brien laughed. "I knew it was too good to be true. Today is the day we're going shopping for your winter clothes, remember?"

Molly groaned. She'd totally forgotten about the planned shopping trip. "Can't we do it another day?" she begged. "I'm supposed to meet Josh."

"You'll have to meet him later," Mrs. O'Brien said, pulling on her own coat. "This is the only time I have to take you, and you've got to get some new jeans and sweaters before your school accuses me of being a neglectful mother."

"But I can't meet him later," Molly said. "He's playing basketball this afternoon. Please, Mom, it's important!"

"So are your new clothes," Mrs. O'Brien said calmly. "Now, why don't you call Josh and tell him you can't make it. Then we'll get going."

So it was that a scowling Molly spent the morning in town with her mother, going from the island's tiny department store to the army-navy store to the shoe store. By the time they were done, it was two o'clock, the library was closed, and Molly owned two new pairs of jeans, two sweaters, three blouses, a denim skirt, and new high-tops. She was fuming. A perfectly good Saturday morning had been wasted.

"One more stop and then we're done," Mrs.

O'Brien said. She parked in front of Cole Antiques. "Mr. Cole has an old sideboard that might be perfect for our dining room."

"I'll wait in the car," Molly said quickly. She wasn't eager to see Mr. Cole.

"Don't be silly! This could take awhile."

"Ah, how are you, Mrs. O'Brien?" Mr. Cole called as they walked in. "Have you heard?"

"Heard what?" Mrs. O'Brien asked.

Mr. Cole's round face was full of excited indignation. "It seems we've got a crime wave on our hands!" he said grandly.

Molly's mother frowned. "What do you mean?"

"Jay Slatkin's grocery store was broken into last night. So was Amital's Bakery!"

Molly's eyes widened. It was rare that there was any crime on Blackberry Island. The place was just too small—everyone knew everyone else.

"Oh, that's too bad," Mrs. O'Brien said. "Did they lose a lot of money?"

Mr. Cole coughed. "Well, in fact, the thief seemed to be after the, ah, food goods."

"Food goods?" Molly echoed, puzzled.

Mr. Cole threw her an irritated look. "Cheese puffs," he said, sounding reluctant. "Several bags of cheese puffs and some grape soda were stolen, I hear. And some pre-made sandwiches."

"Oh, I see." Mrs. O'Brien sounded as if she were trying not to laugh. "How about at Amital's?"

Mr. Cole scratched his cheek. "Nothing taken there," he admitted. "Amital had closed up for the night. The till was empty and there was nothing on the shelves." After a pause, he burst out, "But the point is, some vandal's going around as bold as brass, breaking into people's shops! I tell you, I'm worried. Why, this place is a treasure trove. I certainly hope the sheriff catches that kid soon."

"Kid?" Mrs. O'Brien repeated. "Do they know it was a child?"

"Well, I don't think they're about to arrest anyone, but it stands to reason, doesn't it?" Mr. Cole said. He looked at Molly again. "If I were you, young lady, I'd stop spending so much time with that Goldberg boy. Broken home, you know. Kids like that often end up in trouble."

Indignation flared up in Molly. "Josh would never steal anything!" she said.

Mrs. O'Brien's voice was cold as she added, "Mr. Cole, Josh Goldberg is a lovely boy. Furthermore, I don't think any of us has the right to predict his future for him. Excuse us."

"But the sideboard!" Mr. Cole squeaked as Molly and her mother headed for the door.

"Thank you, I'm not interested," Mrs. O'Brien said.

She started the car, and they drove in silence for a while. Then Molly said, "How could he say those things about Josh? He's awful!"

Mrs. O'Brien sighed. "Molly, try not to let it bother you too much. Vincent Cole is just a silly, gossipy man. I shouldn't have lost my temper with him. It doesn't do a bit of good."

A faint grin crept across Molly's face. "Well, it made me feel better. I'm glad you did it, Mom."

"Oh, come on, Gwen, nothing will happen to you. I just want you to show me exactly where you saw the ghost, okay?"

Gwen folded her arms. "I don't want to go back down there."

"Please, Gwen?" Molly begged. She didn't want to let the whole day go by without learning *anything* new about the McPhail mystery. "If you just show me the place, I'll do the dishes for you on your next dish night."

Gwen said nothing for a moment. Then she looked at Molly out of the corner of her eye. "Will you rake the backyard tomorrow, too?"

Molly groaned. "Gwen!" Then, seeing the stubborn look in her sister's eyes, she sighed. "Okay, okay. I'll rake, too."

"All right," Gwen said, climbing off her bed. "What are we waiting for? Let's go!"

Molly made sure she had the flashlight in her back pocket. Then she and Gwen crept down to the library. From the parlor, they could hear the low murmur of their mother's voice talking to Mrs.

Hewitt. Otherwise, the house was deserted.

"I heard Mrs. Hewitt on the phone while you were out," Gwen told Molly as they walked down the tunnel. "She was talking to Mr. Hewitt's butler or something. She said, 'Please give him this message.' I bet he wouldn't speak to her himself."

"Cold blooded!" Molly said.

"Yeah, I bet he's really mean. Then I heard her make an appointment for him to come here for tea this afternoon."

Molly peered at Gwen. "You heard a lot," she remarked.

Gwen shrugged. "I just—hey!" She broke off and pointed. "Look at that!"

Molly looked. Her jaw dropped. Stretched across the tunnel in front of them, standing as high as Molly's head and barring the way, was a towering pile of rocks.

"Do—do you think the ceiling caved in again?" Gwen asked, with a nervous glance upward.

Molly shook her head, staring at the pile of rubble. "No," she said slowly. "If all this stuff had fallen down, there'd be a big hole." She knitted her brow. "I don't get it."

"Get what?"

"Well . . ." Molly paused, unsure of herself. Then she went on with growing certainty. "The only thing I can think of is that someone put these rocks here."

"Someone put them here?" Gwen whispered.

"You mean, someone like—the ghost?"

"No," Molly said impatiently. "Ghosts can't carry rocks around."

"Are you sure?" Gwen asked. Stepping up to the crude wall, she pulled out a small stone near its base. "They're not all that heavy—"

A rumbling noise shook the tunnel. Molly stared in horror as the wall started to buckle.

And Gwen was right under its shadow.

"Gwen!" Molly shrieked. *"Look out!"*

CHAPTER FIVE

Molly didn't think. She simply threw herself forward, grabbed Gwen's hand, and pulled as hard as she could. Gwen let out a yell of pain and stumbled toward her. Molly fell over backward, pulling Gwen down with her.

"Get back! Back!" Molly yelled, scrambling backwards as fast as she could. "Move, Gwen!"

With a deafening noise, the wall came down. All around Molly was a thunderous clatter, as if some giant had tipped over a jar of enormous marbles. Dust clogged the air and choked her. The flashlight had gone out, and it was pitch dark.

At last it was over. Coughing and gasping, Molly climbed to her feet. "Gwen?" she called.

No one answered. "Gwen!" Molly yelled again,

horror-stricken. *"Gwen!"*

Beside her in the dark, someone sniffled. "Don't yell at me," Gwen's voice quavered. "It wasn't my fault."

"Oh, Gwen," Molly gasped, throwing her arms around her sister. Then Gwen burst into tears.

"Okay, I won't tell Mom and Dad," Gwen said. "But I'm not going down there again, Molly."

"You don't have to," Molly replied. She shivered. "I'm not sure I want to, either."

Somehow the girls had managed to grope their way back to the secret passage in darkness, and Molly had made sure the way was clear before whisking Gwen upstairs to her room. Now they were sitting on Gwen's bed. Gwen was huddled against the headboard, wrapped in her quilt. There was a smear of dust across her cheek, and her eyes were enormous in her white face.

"What I don't understand is how those rocks got there. Or why," Molly added, thinking aloud.

"Why?" Gwen's voice started to rise. "I'll tell you why! It was the ghost of Mary McPhail. She's trying to get us!"

Was it possible? Molly thought about the sweet face of the girl in the photograph. Could Mary McPhail's ghost really be evil?

Outside, she heard the purr of a car's motor and the crunch of tires on gravel. She crossed to Gwen's window and peered down.

An expensive-looking silver car drew to a halt in front of the inn. A chauffeur in a uniform hurried around to the back door on the passenger side and opened it. A tall, thin, elderly man unfolded himself from the car's interior. "It's old Mr. Hewitt," Molly said to Gwen in a hushed voice. "He's here for tea."

She'd seen Edward Hewitt before, but only from a distance. Now she studied him. He looked to be about Grandpa Lloyd's age, but where Grandpa's head was bald and weatherbeaten, Edward Hewitt's was capped by a shock of silver hair. He had a deeply lined face and a large, beaky nose. His mouth was set in a bitter downturned curve. As Molly watched, he shook the chauffeur's hand off his arm and went up the steps.

Gwen joined Molly at the window. "He *looks* mean," she observed. "I'm glad he's not my grand-father."

"*He's* probably glad he's not your grandfather, too," Molly remarked.

Gwen poked Molly in the ribs. "That isn't very nice!" Then she sighed. "I sure wish we could hear what he says to Mrs. Hewitt."

A moment later a man's voice seemed to float out of thin air. "Good afternoon, Elsa," it said in harsh, clipped tones.

For a second Molly's skin crawled. Then she realized what was happening. Gwen's room was directly above the parlor. When the flue to the woodstove was open—as it was now, since Mr. O'Brien had laid a fire in there for the evening—sounds carried right up the chimney and out the vent in Gwen's room.

"You look older," Mr. Hewitt said.

"I am older," Mrs. Hewitt replied dryly. "We haven't seen each other since Jim's funeral. It's been a hard two years, Ed."

"We should leave," Molly whispered, turning toward the door. She felt funny about listening to their conversation this way. "It's private."

Gwen waved her arms frantically. Mrs. Hewitt was speaking again. Molly hesitated.

"Thanks for coming. I'll keep this short," she said. "I know you've never much liked me, Ed, but I just need to know one thing: Do you care enough about your granddaughter to pay her kidnappers to get her back?"

Molly's heart thudded in her chest. There it was. The big question was out in the open. Even though she knew it was wrong to listen, she *couldn't* leave now.

There was a short silence. Then Mr. Hewitt said, "Out of curiosity, what makes you think I don't care about her?"

"His voice is weird," Gwen whispered. "Like he's choking or something."

"Well, for one thing," Mrs. Hewitt replied, "you haven't seen her or spoken to her once since Jim's death. She turned eleven in October, and you didn't even send her a birthday card, for heaven's sake!" She sounded angry now. "If you do care about her, you have a funny way of showing it!"

Molly braced herself for Mr. Hewitt's angry response. But to her surprise, when he spoke again his voice was gentle.

"Does she talk about me?" he asked.

"Not anymore," Mrs. Hewitt answered. "She used to ask why we never saw you, but by now she's got the message, Ed. She knows she's been cut out of your life. She just doesn't know why. For that matter, neither do I."

"Ow," Gwen whispered. Molly looked down and found she was digging her fingers into Gwen's arm. She let go. "Sorry," she whispered.

Then Mr. Hewitt said, "I couldn't, Elsa. I just couldn't."

"Couldn't what?"

"See Carrie," he replied in a muffled voice. "She looks too much like her father. . . . "

There was another silence. When Mrs. Hewitt spoke again her voice had changed, softened.

"Oh, Ed," she said. "That's exactly why you need to see her. *Because* she's Jim's daughter. Yes, he's gone, but look at what a wonderful part of himself he left behind."

"Hmmph," Mr. Hewitt said. But again, it wasn't an angry sound. Molly suspected the elderly man was trying to keep from crying.

"Poor Mr. Hewitt!" Gwen whispered. "I take back the mean things I said about him."

"And think of Carrie," Mrs. Hewitt went on. "It's been a hard time for her, too. Probably even harder than for you or me. She's only a child. She needs to know you still love her."

Mr. Hewitt cleared his throat. "I hate to admit this—but maybe you're right, Elsa."

"He's definitely crying," Gwen whispered.

"I am right," Mrs. Hewitt said. "We need to be a family again, Ed. Will you try?"

"I—I'd like to," Mr. Hewitt said. He paused, then added in a lower voice, "I just hope I get the chance."

CHAPTER SIX

Molly was in the library late that afternoon when Josh stopped by after his basketball game. "Guess what?" he said, looking pleased with himself. "Since you couldn't make it, I went to the library on my own this morning and made copies of a bunch of old newspapers."

"Oh. Okay," Molly said.

Josh frowned. "Well, don't sound so excited," he grumbled. "What's the matter with you, anyway, O'Brien? Why are you acting so gloomy?"

"A lot of weird stuff has happened today," Molly said. She didn't tell him about the incident with Mr. Cole—that would have hurt his feelings. But she did tell him about the talk she and Gwen had heard between Edward and Elsa Hewitt.

"Wow," Josh said when she was done. "So I guess he will agree to pay the ransom, huh?"

"He didn't come right out and say that," Molly admitted. "But I'm sure he meant it." She bit her lip, remembering. "He's not horrible after all, you know. He's really kind of sad."

"Intense," Josh said, shaking his head.

"Yeah," Molly agreed. "And before that there was the collapsing wall in the tunnel."

"What?" Josh demanded.

Molly told him what had happened in the tunnel earlier that day. She was relieved when he agreed with her that a ghost couldn't have built the wall that had nearly crushed them.

"It's impossible," he said. "If there's one thing everyone knows about ghosts, it's that they can't do things like lift rocks—unless they're poltergeists." Suddenly he looked worried. "Mary McPhail's ghost isn't a poltergeist, is it?"

Molly chewed a fingernail. She hadn't thought of that. "I don't think so," she said after a minute. "But I'm not positive."

"Well, I hope she's not," Josh said. He frowned and stood up. "I want to see the wall."

Molly's stomach jumped at the thought of going down there again. "Uh—we can't," she said quickly. "My flashlight broke last time."

"That's all right. I brought mine," Josh said, reaching over and pulling his flashlight out of his backpack.

"Oh." Molly swallowed hard. "Well, okay."

After poking his head around the door to be sure all the adults were elsewhere, Josh signaled to Molly to open the secret passage. As they reached the bottom of the steps he gave Molly a little sideways grin. "I'll go first, if you're scared," he whispered.

"I am not scared!" Molly whispered back angrily. Snatching the flashlight from him, she marched down the tunnel to the pile of rubble.

When he got there, Josh studied the rocks thoughtfully. "Weird," he said after a moment. "Someone must have put these here."

"I know," Molly said. "But who? And where did they come from?"

"Well, there are other branches of the tunnels we can explore," Josh said. He looked at Molly.

After a moment she nodded. "Okay," she said. "Come on."

Picking their way over the rocks, the two friends headed into the maze of tunnels.

Josh led the way. They turned down branch after branch until Molly had no idea which way they were heading anymore.

Some of the ways were blocked by huge, deep puddles. Others ended in barriers of caved-in rubble. A few had been shored up with logs. "These have been here for over a hundred years," Molly said in a hushed voice. She rested her hand on a smooth curved trunk. "I can practically see the smugglers in here, digging the tunnels out by lantern-light, hauling in these big logs. . . . "

"Did you just hear something?" Josh asked suddenly.

Molly's eyes widened. "Like what?"

"Like a splash."

Both of them stood still for a long moment, straining their ears. The sound was not repeated.

Josh shrugged. "I guess it was nothing. Come on, let's keep going."

They walked on in the gloom. But the back of Molly's neck was prickling. Was someone else in the tunnels with them?

They moved past the dark mouth of a passageway. Suddenly, Molly caught a flash of movement out of the corner of her eye. She whipped around and aimed the flashlight down the tunnel.

It shone on a slender hand in a white sleeve, just disappearing at the far end of the passageway.

"Hey!" Molly yelped. She plunged into the tunnel, running toward where she'd seen the hand.

"O'Brien, where are you going?" Josh yelled, pounding after her. "Hey, it's dark back here!"

Molly skidded to a halt at a bend in the tunnel. Cautiously she shone the light around the corner, then peered after it.

In front of her were three tunnels radiating out from the center like the spokes of a wheel. She could see no movement in any of them. As Josh came dashing up beside her, she held up a hand to stem his questions. "Listen," she said.

They listened. And heard nothing. The silence was so complete Molly could almost make out her own heartbeat.

"What's going on?" Josh demanded.

She drew in a deep breath. "I just saw the ghost," she said.

Josh stared. "Are you sure?"

"Yes. She was heading this way," Molly said, indicating the three tunnels with a sweep of her light. "Now she's gone. No live person could have vanished like that, Josh. She . . . dematerialized!"

After a moment Josh shrugged. "Well, maybe she'll materialize again. Anyway, since we're here we might as well check out one of these tunnels. What do you say?"

"Okay," Molly agreed.

This time Molly took the lead. She chose the left-hand tunnel and tramped forward, every sense alert for another sign of the ghost.

Suddenly Josh said, "Stop! Give me that light, O'Brien!"

"What is it?" Molly asked, passing him the flashlight.

Josh aimed it up at the low ceiling of the tunnel. Set into the packed earth was a wooden hatch. "Look at that," he said.

Molly caught her breath. "A trapdoor!"

Josh nodded. "I think we just found another entrance."

"Well, what are we waiting for?" Molly said excitedly. "Let's see where it comes out!"

Since the ceiling there was only a little higher than Josh's head, Molly was able to reach the hatch by standing on her friend's back. The two big bolts that held it closed slid aside with ease. Molly heaved at the hatch, and was startled when the whole thing popped out of place like a manhole cover. Shoving the hatch to one side, she set her hands on the edge of the trapdoor and pulled herself up.

Bong! Her head struck something metal. "Ow!" Molly yelped.

"Shhh!" Josh cautioned from below.

"Easy for you to say," Molly grumbled. Keeping her head low, she squirmed out of the hole and peered around in the gloom.

A bit of light came in from a window set high up in one wall. Molly could see that she'd banged her head on a big metal tank on legs. The trapdoor was directly under it. The air smelled of heating oil.

She stuck her head down through the hole. "I think I'm in someone's basement," she reported. "The tunnel comes out under their oil tank!"

"Look out. I'm coming up," Josh said. Placing his hands on the edge of the hole, he pulled himself up through it with a twisting motion.

"Watch your head," Molly cautioned.

Too late. "Ouch!" Josh hissed. Pulling his legs through the hole, he sat up and rubbed his head. Then he looked down through the trapdoor. "I dropped my flashlight."

"We'll get it on the way back," Molly said.

The two friends looked around. Dusty, shrouded shapes hulked in the gloom. Molly's heart was beating fast. "Josh, are we trespassing?" she whispered.

"It's only trespassing if there's a 'no trespassing' sign," Josh replied. "I think."

Molly wiped her jeans with hands clammy with nervousness and decided it was better not to think about it at all. The important thing was to figure out exactly where they were.

"There are the stairs," she whispered, pointing. "Come on."

Ducking thick, ropy cobwebs, Molly crept up the cellar stairs with Josh at her heels. At the top was a stout door. She pressed her ear against it. She could hear nothing on the other side.

She gulped. "Here goes," she whispered, and turned the doorknob.

The door creaked open into a room filled with more dark shapes. Molly and Josh stepped out, and Josh shut the door behind him. It was dusk by now, and the room was in shadow. Fading sunlight picked up the gleam of polished wood. Molly's gaze swept over a chest of drawers, a table, and a walnut sideboard, all lined up against a wall.

As soon as she saw the sideboard she realized with horror where they were. "Josh!" she whispered frantically. "We're in Mr. Cole's utility room!"

Just then the door that led to Mr. Cole's shop was jerked open. A portly figure stood outlined against the yellow light.

Mr. Cole! He gripped a baseball bat in one hand.

"The police are on their way!" Mr. Cole shouted. "Whoever's there, you might as well give yourself up!"

CHAPTER SEVEN

"Run!" Josh whispered.

At first Molly was frozen to the spot with panic. But as Josh dashed past her and flung open the outer door of the utility room, she snapped out of her daze and raced after him.

"Hey, stop!" Mr. Cole shouted. "Stop, you rotten kids! Come back here! Thieves!"

But Molly and Josh were already pelting through his side yard as fast as they could go.

They tore up Oak Street, turned onto Main, and cut across Founder's Green. Racing across the grass, they flung themselves into a clump of bushes behind the bandstand.

"Do you think he recognized us?" Molly panted.

"I hope not," Josh replied. He braced his hands

on his knees for a moment while he caught his breath. Then he peeked up over the rail of the bandstand. No one seemed to be following them. "I don't think so. It was dark in there."

"He knew we were kids, though," Molly said doubtfully.

"He saw our shadows. We're smaller than adults," Josh pointed out. "It was obvious."

"Yeah, I guess." Molly blew out her breath in a huge sigh. "Boy, for a second there I thought we were dead. Imagine trying to explain to Mr. Cole what we were doing in his utility room!"

"Knowing Mr. Cole, we'd be explaining it to the police," Josh said. "He thought we were there to steal his antiques."

The November evening was on the chilly side. Molly hugged her arms around herself. "Josh," she said thoughtfully, "we did learn something. Whoever put those rocks in the tunnel didn't get in through Mr. Cole's basement. That hatch was bolted from the inside,"

"That's true," Josh agreed. "So I guess we can rule out Mr. Cole."

"Uh-huh," Molly said. "How many people live on Blackberry Island?"

"Around three thousand, I guess," Josh answered. "Why?"

Molly looked glum. "One down," she said. "Two thousand, nine hundred ninety-nine to go."

"Listen to this," Josh said. He read aloud, "'Only the day before the shocking event, the miscreants were overheard in a violent alter—altercation behind a waterfront taproom.'"

Gwen made a face. "'A violent alteration?' What's that supposed to mean?"

"Altercation," Molly corrected. "I think it means a fight."

"Why didn't they just say that, then?" Gwen grumbled. "It's almost like they spoke a different language in the olden days. What's a miscrayon, anyway?"

Molly wasn't about to admit that she didn't know. "Here," she said, handing a paperback dictionary to her sister. "Look it up."

It was just after lunch on Sunday, and Molly, Gwen, and Josh were seated at the table in the library at Welcome Inn. Photocopies of old newspaper articles were strewn around them. They were trying to learn all they could about the trial of John McPhail.

"Boy, this case must have been really big news," Gwen said. "It seems like the local newspapers didn't write about anything else."

"I guess they didn't get a lot of murders here," Molly said. "Okay. So far we know that John McPhail and Martin Ames had a fight the day before Ames was killed."

"We also know that it was McPhail's knife that stabbed Ames," Josh said. He held up a photocopy and tapped it. "It's right here."

"Sounds like McPhail did it," Gwen said.

"Yeah, but at his trial McPhail said—oh, what did he say?" Molly rummaged among the papers for a moment. "Here it is. He said, 'I was using the knife to cut some rope and left it lying in the tunnel where anyone could have picked it up. I did not stab Martin Ames. He was my friend and my cousin.'"

"He couldn't have done it," Josh said. "The most obvious suspect is always innocent. Everyone knows that."

"I know." Molly frowned and wrapped a strand of dark hair around her finger. "Maybe what we should do is try to figure out who *did* do it."

"That'll be hard," Josh said. "Everybody who might know has been dead for years and years."

Molly leaned back in her chair, thinking. "I wonder what that violent altercation was about," she murmured.

"It tells about it right here," Gwen replied, "in this article about the third day of the trial." She handed the page to Molly.

"Hmm," Molly said, skimming the article rapidly. "It started when McPhail asked Ames who they were doing the smuggling for. Ames wouldn't tell him, and McPhail got really mad. McPhail said he threatened not to do the job at all if Ames didn't tell him who they were working for. But then Ames got all upset and said if he ever told anyone who his employer was, the employer would have him killed. He said the employer was a very powerful man."

"What?" Josh sputtered. "Are you serious? You mean someone else threatened to kill Martin Ames, and they still hanged John McPhail for it?"

"Well, they only had McPhail's word that Ames really said that," Molly pointed out. She glanced back at the article. "McPhail told the court that Ames always carried a little black book with all his plans and stuff in it, and that book might have the name of the guy who hired him. But they never found any black book. The judge said afterward that McPhail made it up."

"If we could find that book, I bet we could solve the whole case just like *that*," Gwen said, snapping her fingers.

"Yeah," Molly agreed. "*If* we could find it. But I'm sure it's long gone." She sighed. "Let's keep reading."

A few minutes later Josh started to laugh. "Listen to this," he said. "This article is about the raid on the smugglers' tunnels. 'From start to finish, the operation was a roaring success. The customs agents were much aided in their work by Mayor Whartley. His Honor, in a most uncommon show of zeal for the law, personally took part in the round-up of the criminal gang.'"

"What's so funny about that?" Molly asked.

Josh held up the page he'd been reading. "If Mayor Whartley really looked like this drawing, I'm surprised he didn't get stuck in the tunnels."

Molly and Gwen both peered at the woodcut illustration. Captioned "The Mayor Gets His Man," it showed a round, chubby-cheeked man aiming a pistol at a scowling smuggler.

"I can't even imagine him puffing after the smugglers!" Molly exclaimed, laughing.

"He looks like a bowling ball." Gwen giggled.

Josh shrugged. "I guess you can't always go by what a person looks like. According to this article, the mayor was right in there leading the charge. Also, he's the one who closed off the tunnels afterward. He actually wanted to blow them all up, but after the first dynamite charge leveled some rich guy's house he had to settle for just sealing the entrances. Lucky for us he missed a few."

Gwen shivered. "I don't call it lucky."

"Oh, *no!*" Molly cried. Josh's comment about the tunnel entrances had just made her realize something truly awful.

"What?" Josh and Gwen said together.

Molly stared at Josh, her cheeks pale. "Josh, the hatch in Mr. Cole's basement," she said. "We left it open! What if he goes down there and finds it? Then he'll know how we got in!"

"You're right." Suddenly Josh clapped a hand to

his forehead. "O'Brien, it's worse than that. Remember when I dropped my flashlight?"

Molly gasped. "It's still in the tunnel!"

"And it has my name on it," Josh added. "If Mr. Cole finds it, he'll know exactly who was in his utility room."

He and Molly stared at each other, horrified.

"I'll visit you guys in jail," Gwen offered. "I'll even learn how to bake so I can make you a cake with a file in it."

Then Molly shook herself. "We're not going to jail," she said with determination. "I'm going to get another flashlight from the kitchen. Then we're going back there right now to get Josh's flashlight and close that hatch. Gwen, if Mom or Dad asks where we are, cover for us."

"Okay," Gwen agreed. "What should I say?"

"Make something up," Molly told her impatiently. "Come on, Josh. We've got to move!"

"I don't think Mr. Cole took your flashlight," Molly said, trying to sound sure.

"Well, someone took it," Josh said. "It wasn't where I left it. I wish I believed that ghosts could do things like steal flashlights. I'd rather face Mary McPhail than Mr. Cole any day."

Though they hadn't found Josh's flashlight, Molly and Josh had managed to rebolt the hatch that led into Mr. Cole's basement. Now they were heading back through the tunnels toward the inn.

Molly glanced sidelong at Josh, admiring his calm. If the missing flashlight had had her name on it, she thought, she'd be at the harbor by now, trying to catch the next boat to China.

"I don't think Mr. Cole even looked in his basement," she offered. "The hatch was still exactly the way we left it. It didn't seem as if anyone had been there since yesterday."

"How can you be so sure?" Josh asked.

Molly flushed. "I guess I can't," she admitted. "I just *hope* no one's been there."

"Well, we'll find out soon enough," Josh said with a sigh. "Let's not talk about it anymore, okay?"

They turned right into the main tunnel and scrambled over the remains of the rock wall. As they approached the door that led to the secret passage in the O'Briens' library, Molly suddenly caught sight of a rectangle of white against the dark wood of the door. She touched Josh's arm. "Look," she whispered.

They moved hesitantly forward. Josh put out his hand and picked the white thing up. It was a folded piece of notebook paper that had been stuck between the latch and the door.

Molly watched as Josh slowly unfolded the paper. On it were five lines of writing, all in heavy block letters.

Josh frowned. "It's a note," he said.

"What does it say?" Molly asked. Moving around so she could look over his shoulder, she peered down at the scrap of paper.

This is a warning. You must stay away from the tunnels. If you don't, something very terrible will happen to you. BEWARE!

Then Molly read the signature and gasped. Silently she pointed it out to Josh. He stared at her in absolute astonishment.

"This is *weird*," he whispered.

"I'll say," Molly agreed fervently.

The note was signed, "Your friend, Mary McFail."

CHAPTER EIGHT

"Well, obviously this note isn't *really* from Mary McPhail," Molly said.

"Right," Josh said. "Everyone knows ghosts don't write letters." But he sounded unsure.

"It isn't that," Molly said. Who really knew whether or not ghosts could write letters? "It's the signature. Look. Whoever wrote it spelled 'McPhail' wrong! Not even a ghost would spell her own name wrong."

"I was just going to mention that," Josh said quickly.

Molly raised her eyebrows. Josh wasn't a very good speller, but she didn't say anything.

"You don't think Gwen left this here as a joke, do you?" he asked.

Molly shook her head. "No," she said. "Gwen's a pain sometimes, but she wouldn't do something like that. Also, she knows how to spell McPhail."

"So who sent it?"

"That's a good question," Molly said, nodding. "And what are they up to? Are they the ones who took your flashlight? What for? Where did they come from, what do they know about us, and how do they know we know about Mary McPhail?"

"Those are good questions, too," Josh said. "But there's one question that's even more important," Josh said.

Molly gave him a searching look.

He folded his arms. "Exactly what are they going to do to us if we *don't* keep out of the tunnels?"

At that Molly felt a chill that reached deep down into the pit of her stomach. "Let's get out of here and talk about it somewhere else."

But when they reached the top of the stairs behind the swinging bookshelf, Molly heard Gwen saying, "Sure, Mom, if I see her I'll tell her you're looking for her and you're mad."

"Uh-oh. What do you think that means?" Molly whispered, worried.

Josh spread out his hands. "How would I know? It's your family," he whispered back. "But it didn't sound good, O'Brien."

Molly pressed her ear against the door and listened. When the library remained quiet for a few moments, she cautiously twisted the little knob and the secret door swung out.

Gwen rushed to face them, her face completely serious. "Boy, are you in trouble," she whispered.

"For what?" Molly asked, grabbing her sister's arm.

"I don't know exactly," Gwen said. "But Mr. Cole is here."

Molly gulped. "Oh, no."

"Oh, no," Josh echoed hollowly.

"Oh, yes. I told Mom I thought you went somewhere with Josh, but I didn't know where," Gwen said to Molly. "You guys go out the window. Then come back through the front door and pretend you were outside all the time, Molly. Josh, you better just go home."

"She's right," Molly said as Josh began to protest. "There's nothing you can do."

Josh nodded and picked up his skateboard, which he'd stashed under one of the library chairs. Then he opened one of the tall windows and climbed through it onto the front porch. Molly followed him.

Outside, the friends faced each other. "Good luck," Josh said.

"Thanks," Molly said, feeling forlorn.

"And call me when it's over," he added.

"Okay. See you," she said. Then, squaring her shoulders, she turned and walked into the house.

As she closed the door behind her, Mrs. O'Brien appeared in the dining room doorway. "Molly, would you please come into the study?" she said in a quiet voice.

Molly clenched her sweating hands in the pockets of her sweatshirt. "Sure, Mom," she replied.

Mr. O'Brien was also in the study, waiting for her. His normally cheerful face was grave, his dark eyes solemn. By the window stood Mr. Cole.

"Where have you been?" Mrs. O'Brien asked.

"Uh—out with Josh," Molly said vaguely.

"Hmmph!" Mr. Cole snorted.

"I see. Well, Molly, Mr. Cole has just told us a rather disturbing story about you," Mrs. O'Brien said. "We thought it would be best if you answered his questions yourself, so he can see that it isn't true."

"Oh." Molly tried her best to look innocent. "Uh—okay."

"Believe me, folks, I'm not any happier to be here than you are to have me," Mr. Cole said. But looking at him, Molly didn't believe that.

He faced her. "Do you know why I'm here?"

"No," Molly said. She could guess, of course, but that wasn't the same thing as *knowing*.

"Someone broke into my shop last night," the antiques dealer told her, his voice rising with anger.

Molly widened her eyes. "Really? Did you see who it was?"

"It was dark. All I saw were two shapes," Mr. Cole said. "One was about your size, and one was a little bigger. Fortunately I came along before they had a chance to take anything."

"Wow," Molly said faintly.

"Mr. Cole wonders if it could have been you and Josh. I told him it couldn't possibly have been," Mrs. O'Brien said. "Neither of you would ever pick the lock on someone's back door and try to steal something from them. The idea!"

"Pick the lock on someone's back door?" Molly echoed, puzzled. "But—is that how they got in?"

"How else were they going to do it?" Mr. Cole asked. He folded his arms. "Well?"

"Well, what?" Molly asked.

"Molly, Mr. Cole wants to know what you were doing last night between five and six o'clock," Mr. O'Brien said.

Molly gulped and resolved to tell the truth—at least, as much of it as she safely could.

"I was with Josh," she said. "But I swear—I swear on a stack of Bibles!—that we did not pick the lock on Mr. Cole's back door, and we did not try to steal anything from his shop."

"Can you prove it?" Mr. Cole demanded.

Mr. O'Brien folded his arms and looked at the antiques dealer. "Mr. Cole, our daughter's word is good enough for us. We don't need more proof than that."

"For that matter," Mrs. O'Brien stuck in, "can you prove your shop was even broken into?"

Molly held her breath. If Mr. Cole had found Josh's flashlight, this was when he'd mention it.

But Mr. Cole merely scowled. "I was there," he said angrily. "I saw those little thieves. It's all the proof I need."

"Don't you think you're making a mountain out of a molehill?" Mrs. O'Brien asked. "Nothing was broken, and nothing was taken. Besides, it's rather far-fetched that an eleven-year-old and a twelve-year-old would try to steal antiques. They're only kids, for heaven's sake!"

Mr. Cole's round cheeks quivered with indignation. "Only kids? What else do you think they're going to do when you let them run wild all the time? Kids are behind those break-ins in the village," he sputtered. "I'm warning you, if anything happens again in my shop, it won't be me up here next time. It'll be the sheriff!"

With that, he spun on his heel and marched out of the room. A moment later, they heard the front door slam.

Mr. O'Brien shook his head. "Ever notice that the ones who don't have any kids of their own are the ones who have the most advice on how to raise them?" he murmured to no one in particular.

Laura O'Brien put her hands on Molly's shoulders. "Now that he's gone, would you mind telling us where you were last night?" she asked. "I confess I was a bit concerned when I realized I didn't know."

Molly's heart fell. They hadn't believed her! "I didn't steal anything from Mr. Cole. I didn't!" she said. "And neither did Josh!"

Mrs. O'Brien stared at her daughter. "Of course we know that, Molly," she said gently. "We never for a minute thought you did."

"It's just that we worry when we don't know where you are," Mr. O'Brien put in. "Especially lately."

As her father spoke, Molly realized she'd jumped to the wrong conclusion. Though neither of them said it, her parents were clearly thinking about Mrs. Hewitt, whose daughter had gone out one day and never come home. Molly looked at her shoes, wishing she could shrink into them.

"I'm sorry," she mumbled. "I didn't mean to make you worry about me."

"We know you didn't." Mr. O'Brien crossed the room and hugged his daughter. "Just remember that we do worry."

"Okay." Molly hugged him back, swallowing the lump in her throat. Then she left the study and slowly walked up the stairs to her room.

She was feeling horribly guilty. While she hadn't told her parents any actual lies, she had certainly led them to reach a false conclusion. They believed she hadn't been anywhere near Mr. Cole's shop the night before, when in fact she had been there. You could even say she and Josh had broken in—though, she reminded herself, they certainly hadn't picked the lock, and they also hadn't broken in on purpose.

But none of that changed the fact that her parents had defended her to Mr. Cole and had believed in her, and all the time she had been deceiving them.

By the time Molly threw herself down on her bed, her eyes were full of tears. But before they had time to fall, there was a tap on her door.

"What?" she mumbled.

"Josh is on the phone," Gwen's voice said.

"Coming." Molly swung her legs off the bed and went out into the hall.

Gwen threw her a sympathetic look. "How long are you grounded for?" she whispered.

"I'm not," Molly replied. "I'll tell you about it after I talk to Josh. I need to use your room for a second." She clattered down the stairs to the second floor, where there was a phone on the hall table. Picking it up, she carried it into Gwen's room and shut the door. Then she lifted the receiver. "Hi," she said glumly.

"Mr. Cole was here, too," Josh said. "Before I got home. My mom was really upset." His voice was furious. "O'Brien, he practically accused me of being the one who broke into Slatkin's and Amital's!"

"What?" Molly cried, outraged. "Josh, that's horrible! He's rotten!" She clenched her fists. "I'm going to tell my parents. We have to do something—picket his store!"

"Hold on," Josh said. "It's not that bad. My mom told him off in a major way. Mr. Cole ended up apologizing to her."

"Oh. Well, all right," Molly said, a little more calmly. "Hey, he didn't say anything about the flashlight, did he?"

"No." Josh sighed. "But, still . . . I feel pretty bad about all this, O'Brien."

"Me, too," Molly agreed. "Josh, nothing in this adventure is going right! We still have no idea who really killed Martin Ames; someone is threatening us to keep out of the smugglers' tunnels; and now we're being accused of theft and lying to our parents about it!"

"I know. I've been thinking. . . ." Josh's voice trailed off.

"Thinking what?" Molly asked.

He sighed again. "Maybe this adventure just wasn't meant to be, O'Brien. Maybe we should pay attention to what it said in that note and just forget about the tunnels."

"And forget about Mary McPhail, too?" Molly said, her heart sinking.

"I don't know what else we can do. We haven't gotten anywhere with solving the murder," Josh pointed out.

Molly twisted the phone cord around her wrist. "Maybe you're right. I hate to let her down, but. . ."

"Do you think she'll haunt us?"

"She might," Molly said gloomily. "I would if I were her. But how can we help her? We don't have a single clue."

There was a silence. Then Josh said, "Well, let's meet tomorrow after school and talk about it some more."

"Okay," Molly agreed quickly. She was glad not to have to decide right away. "See you then."

Molly hung up the phone and opened the door to let Gwen in. She described the scene with Mr. Cole, then reluctantly started telling Gwen about her conversation with Josh. She'd just gotten to the part about giving up their adventure when the phone rang again.

"That's probably Joanne," Gwen said, pouncing on the receiver. "Hello?

"Oh, hi," she said a second later, sounding disappointed. "Hold on, she's right here." Handing the phone to Molly, she said, "It's Josh again."

"What's up?" Molly said into the mouthpiece.

"O'Brien!" Josh practically shouted. "I just had the best idea!"

"What?" she asked, holding the phone away from her ear. "Calm down before I go deaf."

"Sorry." Josh lowered his voice. "I was thinking—in one of those articles, John McPhail said

Martin Ames kept all his records and stuff in a little black book, right? And Gwen said if we could find that book, we could probably solve the case, right?"

"Right," Molly said cautiously. "But we don't even know if the book really exists. No one ever found it."

"*That's* what I was thinking about," Josh said. "Supposedly, Ames always carried the book with him. So what if he had it with him when he was killed? And what if it fell out of his pocket, or wherever it was, when he was stabbed?"

"You mean—" Molly began, excited.

"Yeah!" Josh interrupted. He was shouting again. "Maybe that's why they never found it—because the mayor sealed up the tunnels right after the raid. O'Brien, that black book could be down there in the tunnels right now!"

CHAPTER NINE

Molly sucked in her breath. "Are you sure you know what you're saying, Josh?"

"Well, I guess so, since I'm the one saying it," he retorted.

"No, I mean the part you didn't say yet. Do you really want to go back down into the tunnels and look for Martin Ames's book?" Molly asked.

Gwen made a face. "I thought you said we were giving up on that," she whispered.

Molly waved her to silence. "We have to try it, O'Brien," Josh was saying. "If we don't find the book, *then* we can give up. But we have to try."

Molly felt the familiar excitement starting to bubble up inside her again. "I guess you're right," she said.

"I don't believe this," Gwen groaned.

By now Molly had a wide grin on her face. "We couldn't possibly stop now, could we?" she said. "Not when we have the key to the whole mystery practically in our hands."

"Definitely not," Josh said.

"Come on over," Molly told him happily. "And bring those photocopies of the newspaper articles with you. We need to make some plans."

"You'd think they would have drawn a diagram or something to show where Ames was killed," Josh grumbled. "How are we going to find the book without knowing where the body was?"

"That's creepy!" Gwen protested, shocked.

"It is kind of gross, Josh," Molly had to agree. "Anyway, I'm sure the reporters and people like that didn't know how important it was to tell the exact location."

"Well, if I'd been there I would have known it was important," Josh muttered.

It was an hour later that Sunday, and once again Molly, Gwen, and Josh were gathered in the library poring over the photocopied newspaper articles. Each of them had four articles—a third of the whole collection.

"Maybe we can figure it out from other things they say in the articles," Molly suggested. "Like yesterday I read something about how Ames disappeared when the raid started. If we can find out where he was going, that might help us figure out where he went." She bit her lip. "If you know what I mean."

"The way you said it, it doesn't make a whole lot of sense," Josh told her. "But believe it or not, O'Brien, I know exactly what you mean."

"Wow, listen to this!" Gwen said. "'Customs agents were much alarmed to discover that one of the liquor cases contained not rum but a vicious snapping lizard of some six feet in length, apparently a curiosity brought back by one of the villains from the Cayman Islands.' That's mean! Poor lizard. I bet it hated the cold weather up here. I hope somebody found it a nice warm home."

Molly sighed. Gwen sometimes had trouble sticking to the subject.

She skimmed over her articles as fast as she could. "Nearly a hundred and fifty cases of contraband spirits were found. . . ." she read to herself. No, that didn't tell her anything useful.

Suddenly a couple of sentences she had read a moment earlier clicked into place in her mind. Molly ran her finger rapidly back up the column of type until she found what she was looking for. Then she read it out loud.

"'The smuggler's body was found in a tunnel said to lead to a concealed dock. His partners in crime were much put out by this revelation, and one stated that it was "just like that coward Ames" to try to escape to a hidden boat.'" Molly put the paper down. "What does that tell us?"

Gwen knitted her brow. "He had a boat hidden somewhere? Doesn't that mean there must have been another exit to the sea?" Her voice was hesitant. "I mean, where else would he have a boat hidden?"

"Hey, that's right!" Josh cried. "Nice going, Gwen."

Gwen's face turned pink with pleasure.

"If we can just figure out where that other sea exit was, we might be getting somewhere," Molly said excitedly.

"How can we figure that out?" Gwen asked.

"Well, it would probably have to be a harbor or sheltered cove of some kind," Molly said.

Gwen waved her hand in the air. "I know! What about the part of the tunnel that goes on past this house? Isn't that going toward the sea?"

Josh and Molly stared at each other. "She's right again," he said. "We forgot all about that branch of the tunnel. We don't even know where it goes."

Molly nodded. "We'll have to explore it."

"I'm always right," Gwen said smugly. "I'm a straight-A student, you know. Well, almost," she added quickly as Molly raised her eyebrows.

"Still," Josh said after thinking about it for a moment, "I doubt if Martin Ames's escape route was that way. That tunnel leads southeast. There aren't any sheltered coves on the east side of the island until you get to Chapin Bay, and I can't believe the smugglers' tunnels go that far. That's practically all the way to South Light."

"That's a lot of digging," Molly agreed. "Where else might the boat have been hidden?"

Josh jumped up. "You must have a map of the island in here somewhere," he said. "Let's check it out. We can look for likely spots, and then see if the tunnels lead us there."

"There's one there on the wall," Molly said, pointing to an old nautical chart in a frame.

Josh carefully lifted the map down from the wall and carried it back to the table. The three of them bent their heads over it, studying the outline of the island.

Just then Mr. O'Brien stuck his head in through the library door. "Gwen, aren't you supposed to rake the backyard today?" he asked.

Gwen glanced at Molly. "We traded," she said.

"Fine." Mr. O'Brien shrugged. "I don't care who does it, just so long as it gets done today." He withdrew, closing the door again.

Molly glanced at the cuckoo clock on the wall. "Let's hurry," she said.

Suddenly Josh stabbed his finger down on the map. "What about Rocky Point?" he asked, tapping an area of beach at the island's northern tip.

"The place where they're building those new condos?" Molly said, wrinkling her nose. Her mother and Grandpa Lloyd had sent around a bunch of petitions trying to stop the construction, but they'd had no luck. It was due to start that very week.

Josh nodded vigorously. "Exactly. See, there never have been too many houses up at Rocky Point, because it's too hard to dig a foundation in all the rocks there. They're going to blast out the condo foundations with dynamite."

"Wow!" Gwen said.

"Anyway," Josh went on, "up till now there's been nothing there but a quiet little cove. It was never used as a harbor, because of all the shoals. But shoals are no problem for a small boat—such as a one-person sailing dinghy."

"Sounds like a perfect place for someone who doesn't want company," Molly said.

"Yeah," Josh agreed. He gazed at the map again, pursing his lips thoughtfully. "And I think it might be what we're looking for. Remember when we found the peephole inside the statue on Founder's Green?"

Molly and Gwen both nodded.

"And remember how the tunnel led off to the north from there?"

"Not exactly," Molly admitted.

Josh pointed at Founder's Green on the map. "Look. When you were looking out through the statue's eyes, you said you could see the bandstand, right?"

"Right," Molly agreed.

"So that means you were looking west," Josh explained. "The bandstand is west of the statue. And when you were looking west, there was a tunnel that led off to your right. So it was going north. And if you go north from Founder's Green"—he traced his finger in a straight line up the map—"you end up at Rocky Point."

Molly gazed at Josh in surprise. "Wow. You really do have a good sense of direction!"

The door to the library opened again and Mrs. Hewitt walked in with a book in her hand. She stopped, looking startled, when she saw the three faces turned toward her.

"Oh, hello," she said. "I'm sorry to disturb you kids, but I was just—" Suddenly she broke off, peering at Josh. A smile broke over her sad face. "Josh Goldberg, is that you?" she asked.

"Yes," Josh admitted. "Hi, Mrs. Hewitt."

"I haven't seen you since you were eight," she said. "My, you've grown!"

"Yeah, well, I guess that happens." Josh seemed embarrassed. "Uh—how are things, Mrs. Hewitt? Is there—is there any news?"

Mrs. Hewitt's smile faded and the sad look came back. She shook her head. "I haven't heard a thing," she said, a tremor in her voice. "Carrie's grandfather and I have been waiting for a call, but it hasn't come." She took a deep breath. "I—I don't quite know what to do next. I guess I'll go back home and wait by the phone."

"Are you leaving Blackberry Island?" Molly asked.

Mrs. Hewitt nodded. "I'm going to Carrie's grandfather's for tea, and then I'm catching the six o'clock ferry. I've already checked out." She held up the book. "I just came to put this back."

"Well, it was sure nice to see you again, Mrs. Hewitt," Josh said awkwardly. "I hope . . . I hope everything turns out all right."

"Yeah," Molly and Gwen echoed.

Tears rose in Mrs. Hewitt's eyes. "Thanks, kids. I hope so, too."

She set the book on the table and quickly left the room.

When the door closed, Gwen sighed. "I feel so sorry for her," she said. "I didn't know I'd ever feel this sorry for a grown-up."

"I wish there was something we could do to help," Molly said.

"Me, too," Josh muttered angrily. "I'd like to tell those kidnappers a thing or two."

The three of them stood there in silence for a moment. Then Molly clapped her hands and made an effort to sound brisk. "We'd better head down into the tunnels if we're really going to do this," she said. "Gwen, if Mom or Dad comes looking for us, will you cover for us again?"

"Cover for you?" Gwen repeated. "I'm coming with you!"

Molly was surprised. "But you hate the tunnels," she said. "You said you'd never go back down there."

Gwen shrugged. "I changed my mind. Besides"— she put her hands on her hips— "if that person who built the wall and left the scary note is down there, you two are going to need me to protect you."

Josh grinned. After a second Molly did, too. "Okay," she said. "Is the coast clear? Then let's go!"

As Molly went down the stone steps and through the door at the bottom, she was struck by how familiar the action was becoming. "I can't believe I only found the secret passage two days ago," she whispered. "I feel like I've done this a thousand times!"

"Me, too," Josh whispered back. "It's weird."

They turned right, heading north in the main tunnel. "Why are we whispering?" Gwen whispered.

Molly hadn't really thought about it. But now that she did, she realized it was a good idea. "If whoever left the note is hanging around down here, we don't want him to hear us," she explained.

"Right," Gwen said promptly. "Everyone, shut up!"

The three of them walked along in silence. Molly held the flashlight, and its yellow beam danced over the rough-hewn walls in front of them. After a while the quiet began to get to them. Molly found she was stepping as lightly as she could, taking care to set her feet down without shuffling, stepping over puddles rather than splashing through them. Picking her way over the rubble from the rock wall, she headed down the first branch. Left. Right. Left again.

Then they were in the tunnel under Founder's Green. Molly aimed the flashlight down the straight path in front of her—and stopped short. Her breath caught in her throat.

Climbing down the ladder from the founder's statue was a thin, white-clad figure. The ghost!

Behind Molly, Gwen squeaked, "Oh, no!"

The figure on the ladder swung around, startled, at the sound. Molly found herself staring full into her face.

She had curly blond hair and big blue eyes in a rather dirty face. Her clothes, too, were smudged and soiled. They were white, Molly saw. White—and modern: a sweatshirt and jeans.

The ghost dropped to the floor and faced them. Molly took a step forward, her thoughts in whirling confusion. "Molly, don't!" Gwen cried, grabbing at her sister's arm.

Josh came up beside Molly, and she glanced

swiftly at him. He was staring at the ghost, his face puzzled. "I know you," he said. Then his eyes widened. "I know you!" he repeated.

The ghost glared at the three friends. Then her finger rose until she was pointing straight at them. "This is your last warning. Get out, or you will regret it!" the ghost cried. "I am the ghost of Mary McPhail!"

"No, you're not," Josh said. "You're Carrie Hewitt."

CHAPTER TEN

For a moment there was utter silence in the tunnel. Then Molly, Gwen, and the ghost all started talking at once.

"*What?*" Molly demanded.

"You mean that's not a ghost?" Gwen cried.

"I don't know what you're talking about," the ghost said nervously. "Who's Carrie Hewitt? I never heard of her."

"This is Carrie Hewitt?" Molly said to Josh.

"I am not!" the ghost insisted.

"Carrie," Josh said. "We grew up together. I may not have seen you since you were seven, but I still recognize you."

"But what's she doing here?" Molly asked Josh. "I don't get it."

He spread out his hands. "Me, neither."

"Wait a minute. I thought she was the ghost," Gwen said plaintively. "Where's the ghost?"

"Hello!" the girl—Molly decided it was silly to think of her as a ghost anymore—called in a sulky voice. "I'm right here, you know. Stop calling me 'she'! I hate it when people talk about me like I'm not there."

"Same old Carrie," Josh muttered. "Spoiled brat."

"I heard that, Josh Goldberg."

"Hold everything!" Molly yelled.

Everyone stared at her in surprise. Molly paced toward the strange girl. "You are Carrie Hewitt, aren't you?"

The girl looked at her feet and said nothing.

"And you're also our ghost," Molly went on, her thoughts churning.

"Huh?" Gwen said.

"We never did see Mary McPhail's ghost," Molly explained to her sister. She felt a weight of sadness settle on her as she said the words. "When you spotted Carrie two days ago, we all thought it was the ghost you saw. It was an easy mistake. Carrie is the right size, she has blond hair like Mary, and she's dressed in white. And we were all sort of expecting to see Mary," she finished in a low voice.

"You mean there's no ghost here?" Gwen asked.

Molly lifted her shoulders. "I guess not."

"Would you guys forget about the ghost for a second?" Josh said. His voice was strained. "I think it's more important to figure out who built that rock wall and left the threatening note."

Molly caught her breath. For a moment she'd totally forgotten that Carrie was being held captive down here.

"The kidnappers!" she said, turning to Carrie. "They must have heard us talking about Mary McPhail. That's why they left that note from her. Only they spelled her name wrong, so we knew it wasn't really from her. It was the kidnappers, wasn't it?"

"Where are they?" Josh demanded. "Are there many of them?"

"Are they mean?" Gwen chimed in.

Carrie's face was blank. "Kidnappers?" she repeated.

Josh and Molly exchanged puzzled glances. It was Molly who caught a glimpse of the truth first.

"You mean you weren't kidnapped?" she said slowly.

"Who says I was?" Carrie demanded.

"Everybody!" Gwen exclaimed. "It's been all over the news for *days!*"

"Really?" Carrie said. The beginnings of a smile formed on her lips. "On TV and everything?"

"TV, radio, the *Island Times*," Josh said. "I think there was even an article about you in the *New York Times*."

"*Really?*" Carrie said again, in a delighted voice.

"Yes, really," Josh said.

"Everyone's been so worried about you, Carrie," Molly added. "Your mother is a wreck! She's going to be so happy to see you safe and sound."

Carrie's face darkened. "No, she won't," she said. "I'm not going back home."

Molly, Josh, and Gwen all exchanged glances. Molly was starting to get the idea that everything about Carrie Hewitt was bound to be surprising.

She sat down on the cool, hard-packed earth, crossed her legs, and set the flashlight on the floor in front of her with the beam shining up at the tunnel ceiling. "Maybe you better start from the beginning," she suggested. "Did you run away from home?"

Carrie nodded.

"But *why?*" Josh asked. He sat down across from Molly.

"I didn't like it there," Carrie muttered. "I hated my school, I hated my house, and I hated my mom."

Molly and Josh glanced at each other again. Carrie didn't look up.

"I wanted to come live with my grandfather, here on the island," she went on. "Everything was fine until we left here. I had my very own pony, you know. Shadow. I kept him at Grandpop's. I got to play on the beach and go outside any time I wanted to. And my mom didn't have a stupid career."

"What does she do?" Gwen asked, interested.

"She's a manager of a big store."

"I don't see what's so stupid about that," Gwen murmured.

"You don't know anything," Carrie retorted. "She works all the time and never thinks about anything else, and we never have enough money." She scowled. The shadows thrown by the upward-pointing flashlight gave her face an eerie, ferocious look. "It wasn't like this when my dad was still alive."

No one knew what to say. After a short silence Josh cleared his throat.

"How did you get here?" he asked.

"It wasn't too hard," Carrie said. "I had saved up my allowance for a while. I took a train to the ferry, and then I got on the ferry with a big group of kids. I think they were on a class trip or something. No one noticed me."

"And how'd you end up in the tunnels?" Josh pressed.

Carrie shrugged. "I've known about them for years. There's an entrance on Grandpop's land."

An entrance on the Hewitt estate! "So that's where the tunnel goes," Molly said.

"It dead-ends under the gazebo," Carrie said, nodding. "I found the entrance the summer before we moved to Connecticut." She glanced at Josh. "I was going to tell you about it back then, but you were mean to me, so I didn't."

Josh flushed. "You were pretty bratty yourself. Anyway, we found it on our own."

"I wonder why the tunnel goes there," Molly mused. "Why would the smugglers want to go to the Hewitt estate?"

"It wasn't the Hewitt estate back then," Carrie pointed out. "It belonged to some guy named Warthog, or something like that. Maybe he was one of the smugglers. Who cares?"

Molly was starting to get annoyed with Carrie, but she kept quiet.

"Okay, so you knew about the tunnels," Josh said. "But how come you've been hiding out in them for almost a week? If you came here to be with your grandfather, why aren't you with him?"

"I went there to see him," Carrie admitted. "But the whole house was dark, and the car wasn't in the garage. There was no one home." Her gaze slid away from Josh's and she started rolling a loose pebble around with her sneakered toe. "And then I kind of changed my mind."

"What do you mean?" Gwen asked.

Carrie leaned against the ladder and put one foot up behind her. She picked at a frayed spot on her jeans, her face wooden. "I didn't know whether he'd want me to stay or not," she said. "I hadn't seen him in a long time. Maybe—maybe he wouldn't have any room for me in the house."

"That place has ten bedrooms!" Josh objected.

"He might have had lots of guests!" Carrie answered angrily.

"But—" Molly started to say. She was going to add *you said there wasn't anyone there.* Before the words left her lips, though, Carrie's glare stopped her. Obviously, Carrie didn't want to explain herself.

"So you came down here into the tunnels," Molly prompted. "And when we started coming down here, too, you tried to scare us away with the threatening note and the wall."

Gwen's eyes narrowed as she suddenly made the connection. "You built that rock wall?" she demanded. "We nearly got killed when it collapsed!"

"I just wanted to keep you out of the part of the tunnels where I was hiding," Carrie said. "I spent all night piling up those rocks." She swallowed hard. "I didn't know they'd fall down like that. I didn't mean to hurt anyone. I'm sorry."

"Yeah, well," Gwen muttered.

"How have you been getting by all this time? Where do you sleep? What have you been eating?" Josh asked.

Carrie's expression grew defiant again, and she said nothing. Suddenly Molly knew why.

"Let me guess," she said. "Cheese puffs and grape soda?"

Carrie's mouth fell open. After a second she gasped, "How—how did you know that?"

"You're the one who broke into the grocery store

and Amital's Bakery, aren't you?" Molly said. "You're the Blackberry Island thief!"

"What?" Josh looked outraged. "You mean I've been getting blamed for what *you* did?"

"I was starving," Carrie muttered. "I'll pay them back someday. Anyway, I didn't even get anything at the bakery. The shelves were bare. I took a flashlight from a drawer, but the batteries died yesterday."

"Hey! Did you take my flashlight?" Josh asked, leaning forward excitedly.

"Well, it was just lying there on the ground," Carrie defended herself. "You can't call it stealing."

"I'm not," Josh said, laughing. "Believe me, I'd much rather you found it than anyone else."

"Huh?" Carrie, looking puzzled, opened her mouth. Then suddenly she shut it again. A knowing smile settled on her lips.

"How'd you get into the stores without anyone seeing you?" Molly asked.

"All the backyards on that street have low fences between them. It's easy to break in from the back if you can get there in the first place. I went up through the basement of that antique shop," Carrie explained. "The same one you guys went into. Yes, I saw you," she added. "And if you tell on me about being here, I'll tell on you about that. I'll say you were the ones who broke into those stores."

Molly and Josh looked quickly at each other. Molly doubted Carrie would get anyone to believe her, but it was possible. She wasn't sure she wanted to take the risk.

"You're not very nice," Gwen said. "We're just trying to help."

"I don't need any help!" Carrie flashed.

"Carrie, why don't you want to go back to your mom?" Josh asked, leaning forward earnestly. "She really misses you."

"She does not," Carrie said. "She doesn't care about me. All she cares about is that dumb store."

"You're wrong," Molly said.

"Yeah," Gwen said. "You should see her. She's been crying all week."

"She's here?" Carrie went pale.

"She's staying in our inn," Molly told her. "She came to the island to see your grandfather."

"See, when everyone thought you had been kidnapped, they were waiting for him to get a ransom note. Only your mom was afraid he wouldn't want to pay the ransom," Gwen chimed in.

Carrie flinched.

"But he said of course he would," Molly added hastily. "He's really worried, too."

"It was really sad," Gwen said. "Molly and I heard the whole thing. By the time they were done talking they were both crying."

"I don't believe you," Carrie said. "My grandfather never cries! He didn't even cry at my dad's funeral. And he doesn't talk to my mom, either, so I know you're making it up."

"Oh, no, we're not," Gwen said.

"They had a meeting yesterday in our parlor," Molly explained. "They made up. They're friends now, Carrie."

"Why are you lying to me?" Carrie burst out angrily. "My mom and my grandfather haven't spoken for two years! They hate each other." She sat down abruptly. "And they don't want me!" Suddenly she burst into tears.

Molly turned to Josh, horrified. He shook his head and shrugged.

"Everything we told you is true, Carrie," Molly said. "Your mother and grandfather do want you back. I know you don't believe me, but if you could just see them—"

Suddenly she broke off as an idea came to her. "Josh, what time is it?" she asked urgently.

He held the flashlight to his watch. "Ten of five. Why?"

"Uh-oh! You never raked the backyard," Gwen reminded Molly. "You're in trouble."

"Never mind about the backyard," Molly said impatiently. She scrambled to her feet, brushing dust off her jeans. "We've got to get to Mr. Hewitt's house before Mrs. Hewitt leaves!"

Carrie's head jerked up. "I told you, I'm not

going home with her! She doesn't want me. So don't try to make me go."

"You don't have to talk to them. They won't even know you're there if you don't want them to," Molly told her. She laid a hand on Carrie's arm. "I just want you to see them so you'll know we're telling the truth."

Carrie wiped her eyes on her sleeve and glared at Molly. "How can I see them without them seeing me?" she asked suspiciously.

"We'll go through the tunnels and out through the gazebo on your grandfather's land," Molly said. "We can find someplace near the front door to hide and you can see your mom when she leaves."

"I don't know," Carrie said, sniffling.

"What could it hurt?" Josh said. He stood up, too, and held out his hand. "Come on, Carrie."

She sat there for a minute, staring down at her hands while the others waited anxiously. Finally she glanced up. "Okay," she said. "I'll look."

"Great! We better hurry. Carrie, you lead the way since you know where you're going," Molly said. She handed Carrie the flashlight.

Carrie certainly did know where she was going. She led them through the tunnels' twists and turns without hesitation. Sooner than Molly expected, they were hurrying down the main branch, past the door that led to Welcome Inn.

The south end of the tunnel had none of the

branches or kinks of the northern part. It led on in a straight line, sloping very gently up, for a quarter of a mile past the inn. Then, abruptly, it ended. A ladder set into the earth wall at the end led up to a hatch like the one under Mr. Cole's cellar. Carrie swiftly climbed up and pushed the hatch aside. And then, one by one, they crawled out into the damp, leaf-scented gloom under old Mr. Hewitt's gazebo.

In front of them, surrounding the gazebo, was a painted-white latticework of wood. It was broken in one place, with a gap big enough to crawl through. Beyond the lattice, across a broad expanse of lawn, lay Mr. Hewitt's house.

They had arrived just in time. Through the lattice, Molly saw Mr. Hewitt and Carrie's mother coming around the corner of the big white house, heading for the garage. Their voices carried clearly across the quiet lawn.

"Charlie will drive you to the ferry," Mr. Hewitt was saying to his daughter-in-law. "You'll be home in three hours. And, Elsa, call me as soon as you have any news."

Molly snuck a glance at Carrie, who was lying belly-down beside her. Carrie's face was pale and strained.

"The minute I hear it," Mrs. Hewitt said. Then her voice cracked. "If only there were some news! It's been six days! I'm beginning to—"

"Don't," Mr. Hewitt said, patting her shoulder. "We'll get her back, Elsa."

Mrs. Hewitt squared her shoulders and nodded. There was a sniffle beside Molly. "I'm going out there," Carrie whispered, and started through the gap in the lattice.

Behind her, Molly, Josh, and Gwen silently gave one another the thumbs-up.

Neither Mr. Hewitt nor Elsa Hewitt noticed as Carrie crawled out from under the gazebo and stood up. She advanced hesitantly over the lawn. "Mom?" she said. "Grandpop?"

Two faces turned toward her, and two sets of eyes stretched wide in disbelief. There was a moment of shocked silence.

"It's me," Carrie said uncertainly.

Then Mrs. Hewitt was running across the lawn toward her daughter.

"Carrie!" she called. "Oh, *Carrie!*"

CHAPTER ELEVEN

"Molly, you're walking so slowly," Gwen complained. "What's the matter with you?"

Molly sighed. "I don't know," she said. "I just feel kind of—blah."

"Are you sick?" Gwen asked. "Don't breathe on me!" Then she reconsidered. "Actually, do breathe on me. I have a spelling test tomorrow."

"I'm not sick," Molly said. "I'm just thinking, that's all." She sighed again.

It was Monday, and the girls were walking home from school. Molly was feeling strangely let down, and she wasn't sure why.

It wasn't that she didn't feel happy for Carrie and the Hewitt family. She did. She had felt especially glad, if a little embarrassed, when Carrie's mother had called Welcome Inn on Sunday night to thank the girls for what they'd done. The happiness in Mrs. Hewitt's voice had given Molly a warm feeling.

Molly, Gwen, and Josh hadn't stayed to watch the whole reunion. Though Gwen had wanted to, Molly and Josh had felt that it should be a private moment. So they'd quietly climbed back down the ladder into the tunnels and gone back to Welcome Inn.

"I can't believe you didn't get into trouble for not raking the lawn," Gwen said now with an envious look. "Some people have all the luck."

"I guess Mom and Dad thought finding Carrie Hewitt was a good excuse," Molly said. She shifted her heavy school knapsack on her shoulders. "But Mom still gave me a lecture about being more responsible and not doing dangerous things like going into tunnels that might be unsafe."

"Well, she's right," Gwen said primly.

Molly snorted. "Gwen, don't be like that! You were just as excited about the tunnels as I was, at least at first."

"Not once I found out there was a dangerous ghost in them!" Gwen retorted. "We're just lucky there was no ghost, that's all!"

"That doesn't make any sense," Molly muttered, rolling her eyes. But there was no real irritation in her voice, because Gwen had just put her finger on what it was that was bothering Molly. It was the fact that their ghost had ceased to exist.

Molly had been so excited when they first spotted what they thought was the spirit of Mary McPhail. And, in spite of all the problems they'd run into while trying to solve the mystery, Molly had always felt buoyed by the thought that they had a real reason for what they were doing. Even when she was feeling really terrible after the trouble with Mr. Cole, she'd thought that in a way it had been worth deceiving her parents, because she was doing it for a good cause.

But now the cause was gone. Molly, Josh, and Gwen had done all that work and gone to all that trouble to help someone who didn't even exist. There was no ghost of Mary McPhail.

The girls turned left and began to trudge up the steep driveway of Welcome Inn. "I can't wait to see what Mr. Hewitt's house looks like on the inside," Gwen said, skipping ahead of her sister. "I'm so glad they invited us over there for dinner tonight. I wonder if he has a swimming pool. Molly, what are you going to wear? Do you think we should dress up? I could wear my new red dress."

"*I'm* not wearing a dress," Molly retorted. She hated wearing anything other than jeans. "You can do what you want. I don't care."

"Well, you don't have to bite my head off," Gwen said, looking hurt. "You really are in a bad mood."

"I'm not!" Molly scowled. When she was in a

bad mood, there was nothing she disliked more than having someone tell her that.

When they reached the big old house, they found Grandpa Lloyd waiting for them in the kitchen. "Hello, youngsters," he greeted them. "Your mother's stuck at her office working late, and your father's out shopping for supper for tonight's guests. So I'm the deputy in charge of making sure that yard finally gets raked."

Gwen and Molly both groaned.

"It's Molly's job to do the raking," Gwen complained. "We traded."

"Well, a trade's a trade," Grandpa Lloyd said, stroking his beard. "But I guess that means you'll be going to the Hewitts' by yourself, Gwen. That yard's going to take your sister a mighty long time if she's got to do it all herself."

Gwen shot Molly a dirty look. "See?" she said. "Some people have all the luck."

"Come on," Molly said, grinning. "Let's get the rakes."

An hour later they put the rakes back into the toolshed and headed indoors. The work had lifted Molly's spirits a little, but she still felt restless. When the girls got inside, she headed for the library.

"Where are you going?" Gwen cried. "We have to get ready to go!"

Molly checked at her watch. "Gwen, we don't have to be there until six o'clock. That's almost an hour from now! I just want to look at something in the library. Don't worry, I'll be ready when it's time to go."

Gwen gave Molly a disbelieving look and headed for the kitchen.

Alone at last, Molly went into the library and shut the door behind her. After a moment's hesitation, she went over to the bookshelf that held the Bible with the red leather cross on the cover. She pulled the book off its shelf, carried it to the table, and set it carefully down.

She opened the front cover. Inside lay the envelope holding John McPhail's last letter to his daughter, on top of the photograph of Mary McPhail and her father. Molly balanced the envelope on her palm for a moment, lightly stroking the mottled old paper with her fingertips. Then she laid it aside and picked up the photograph.

John McPhail's careworn face frowned out at her. He was hanged, she thought with a shiver. What had really happened that night in the smugglers' tunnels? Who had really killed Ames? They'd never know now—there was no longer any reason to find out the truth.

Molly's gaze moved down to Mary McPhail. The big, soulful eyes looked back at her. Once again she felt that somehow, she and Mary McPhail knew each other.

Sighing, she replaced the photograph in the Bible and closed the book's cover. She glanced at her watch again. Five-fifteen. There was time for a quick walk through the tunnels if she felt like it. And she didn't have to be secretive about it this time. Now the whole family knew about the secret passage.

Molly hesitated only a moment longer. Then she picked up the flashlight from the chair where she had left it the day before. She went over to the secret panel and pulled on the black book. The panel swung open and she ran lightly down the stone steps. Another moment and she was in the tunnel.

At least by now she knew her way around reasonably well, Molly reflected. Fifteen minutes later, she arrived at the ladder under Founder's Green. Climbing its rungs, she gazed out for a while through the peepholes in Jan van Huyten's eyes. Across the green, people hurried up and down Main Street. A couple of people were sitting on the steps of the bandstand, but the weather was finally starting to turn chilly, and they didn't stay long. Molly wondered if they had any idea they were being spied on.

But her heart wasn't really in the spying. Somehow, today, the tunnels didn't hold any of their old feeling of promise, of magic.

Frowning, Molly climbed down the ladder again. She checked her watch. Twenty-five to six! She'd better get back. She'd just have time to wash her face and hands before it was time to leave for the Hewitts'. Glancing critically down at her soil-smudged sweatshirt, she realized that she'd better put on a clean shirt and sweater, too.

As she was hurrying toward home, a shimmer of movement at the edge of her flashlight beam caught her eye. A rat? No, it was bigger than that. . . .

Aiming the light down the long shaft of the tunnel, she was just in time to see blond hair and a white sleeve disappearing around a corner.

"Carrie!" Molly called. "Wait up!" She ran to the curve and rounded it. What was Carrie doing down here?

When Molly aimed her beam up the intersecting tunnel, though, she couldn't see anyone. Puzzled, she turned and flashed it the other way. And there was Carrie, already far down the shaft, hurrying as fast as she could go in the opposite direction from her grandfather's house.

"Carrie!" Molly yelled again, but she didn't turn around. Shaking her head, Molly decided not to go after her. If Carrie didn't mind being late for dinner at her grandfather's, that was her business. Molly, however, planned to be on time. She glanced at her watch again and gasped. Ten to six!

She ran the rest of the way to the inn and panted up the stairs into the library at five of. She dashed upstairs to her room, quickly threw on a clean flannel shirt and a cotton sweater, ran into the bathroom, washed her hands, and splashed water on her glowing face. Then she clattered down the two flights of stairs to the front hall.

Gwen was waiting by the door, decked out in her new red dress, blue tights, and her usual tangle of strange jewelry. "We're going to be late," she said accusingly to Molly. "Or we would, except that Grandpa Lloyd said he'd drive."

"Sorry," Molly panted.

Outside a horn honked. The two girls hurried out and piled into Grandpa Lloyd's ancient pickup truck.

"All aboard," Grandpa called, and then steered the truck down the hill to the road. Three minutes later, just as Molly was beginning to get her breath back, they pulled into the driveway of Mr. Hewitt's big white house.

Grandpa Lloyd sat in the truck watching while Molly and Gwen went up and rang the doorbell. Old Mr. Hewitt himself opened the door. He greeted Molly and Gwen with a smile. Then he caught sight of Grandpa in the truck. His eyes narrowed.

"Is that you, Lloyd Foster?" he called.

"It's me," Grandpa replied.

"Well, why are you sitting there?" Mr. Hewitt said. "Come on inside and stay for supper!"

A startled-looking Grandpa climbed out of his truck and walked up to the porch. "Ed, are you feeling all right?" he asked. "Last time we spoke, you told me to go to blazes."

"Well, let's just say I *wasn't* feeling all right then.

I'm better now," Mr. Hewitt said. He gave a lop-sided smile. "All right by you?"

Grandpa Lloyd chuckled. "Fine by me," he said. "I'd be pleased to stay for supper."

"Good!" Mr. Hewitt said heartily. "Come in!"

Molly and Gwen looked around with wide eyes as they followed Mr. Hewitt through a lofty, stone-floored foyer.

"Where's the butler?" Gwen whispered to Molly.

Mr. Hewitt overheard her and laughed. "It's his night off," he said. He led them into a spacious, luxuriously furnished living room. Picture windows showed a wide expanse of twilit lawn, sloping down to a tangle of trees and, beyond that, the gray Atlantic Ocean.

Josh was already there with his mother. Molly and Gwen's parents had been invited, too, but they couldn't take the night off from the inn.

"Where's Carrie?" Molly asked Josh. "Did she make it back yet?"

"Back from where?" Josh asked.

At that moment, Carrie herself came into the room with her mother. She was wearing a new-looking pair of corduroy pants and a blue blouse. Her face was clean and her curly blond hair was brushed into a neat braid. Gone was the sullen, unhappy expression; now her face wore a tentative smile. "Hi," she said in a shy voice.

"Hey!" Josh, Molly, and Gwen all chorused at once. They hurried forward to greet her.

"Wow!" Molly said. "How'd you get back here and change so fast?"

"What are you talking about?" Carrie asked.

"I saw you in the tunnels ten minutes ago, still wearing those white clothes," Molly told her. "Didn't you hear me calling you?"

Carrie was staring at her. "I wasn't in the tunnels ten minutes ago," she said. "I haven't gone back down there since I came out yesterday."

"Come on," Molly said, a little annoyed. "Stop kidding, Carrie. I saw you!"

"I'm not kidding! Ask my mom—we've been baking cookies for the last hour." Carrie shivered. "After the week I spent there, I don't care if I never go down in those tunnels again!"

Molly frowned, confused. "But . . ." Suddenly her eyes widened.

"O'Brien," Josh said. "Are you thinking what I think you're thinking?"

"I think so," Molly answered. She turned to him with shining eyes. "Josh, don't you see what this means?"

"We were wrong before," Josh cautioned.

"But not this time," Molly said. She was filled with a feeling of certainty. "This time I know we're right."

"Right about what?" Carrie asked.

"The ghost of Mary McPhail," Molly said. "She really is down there after all!"

CHAPTER TWELVE

"Are you kidding?" Carrie cried.

"Not again," Gwen groaned.

"Shh!" Molly said, glancing over at the adults. Luckily, they were all talking animatedly and didn't seem to have noticed the outburst.

"We have to go back into the tunnels!" Molly announced in a low voice.

"I'm not going back down there," Carrie protested.

"All right, *you* don't have to," Molly told her. "But I do. Mary McPhail's ghost is still waiting for someone to clear her father's name. She probably thinks we've forgotten all about her by now, and just when we were so close to finding out the truth."

"We don't know that," Josh objected.

"We *were* close," Molly argued. "I know we were on the right track when we thought of looking for that little book. We shouldn't have given up."

Josh was opening his mouth to say something when suddenly his expression changed. He clapped a hand to his forehead. "Holy cow!" he said.

"What?" Gwen pressed.

"There's something I forgot to tell you guys," Josh said, looking from Molly to Gwen. "I skateboarded up to Rocky Point this afternoon. They started blasting the foundation for the condos today."

In another moment Molly saw what he was getting at. Her heart jolted within her. "Holy cow is right," she said.

"I don't get it," Gwen complained.

"If Martin Ames's black book really is in the tunnels near Rocky Point, we're in trouble," Molly explained. "The blasting could make the tunnels around there collapse, just like they did when the mayor tried to blow up the tunnels a hundred years ago. Then we'll never find the book!"

"What are we going to do?" Gwen asked anxiously.

"There's only one thing to do." Molly turned to Carrie. "When is dinner being served?"

"Seven-fifteen," Carrie replied.

"That's over an hour from now!" Molly nodded with satisfaction. "Plenty of time. We need some excuse to go out to the gazebo."

Carrie nodded. "Wait here and I'll tell them I'm going to give you all a tour of the estate."

"You mean we're going down there right now?" Gwen quavered. "At night?"

Molly looked at the frightened expression on her younger sister's face and took pity on her. "I think you should stay up here. Somebody needs to keep Carrie company. And if the grown-ups come looking for us, they'll see you two and they won't get suspicious."

Gwen seemed relieved. "Okay, I'll do that."

Just then Carrie rejoined them. "Let's go," she said.

The four kids trooped outside and around the side of the house. Then, while Carrie and Gwen kept an eye on the windows to make sure no one saw them, Molly and Josh crawled under the gazebo. Carrie told them how to open the hatch from the outside. Finally, she reached through the gap in the lattice and handed Molly a black flashlight.

"Be careful," she warned. "I think the batteries are almost dead."

"Hey, that's mine," Josh muttered, looking at the tape around the end of the handle.

"Thanks," Molly said to Carrie. "We'll be back by seven-fifteen, no matter what."

She followed Josh down the ladder, and they started off.

"We don't really have that much time, you

know," Josh said. "It's six-twenty now. It'll take us twenty minutes just to get to Founder's Green from here, and then another twenty to get back. That gives us"—he peered at the glowing face of his watch— "fifteen minutes to get to Rocky Point and search for the book."

"That isn't much time," Molly agreed. "Let's run!" The two of them set off at a fast jog.

Molly was a fast runner over short distances, but she wasn't much good at keeping up a steady pace. By the time they reached the branching part of the tunnel her breath was coming in painful gasps. It didn't help that the tunnel floor was uneven and treacherous. After a minute or two she dropped to a walk, her hand pressed against a stitch in her side.

"I can't . . . run . . . anymore," she gasped. "Sorry."

"That's okay," Josh said generously.

They continued at a fast walk, twisting and turning through the tunnels. Molly kept a sharp eye out for Mary McPhail, but the ghost didn't put in an appearance. "I wonder if she's shy of you," Molly said thoughtfully to Josh.

He looked scornful. "Women," he muttered.

Finally they reached Founder's Green. The tunnel that ran north from there was one they hadn't explored at all. It looked dark and threatening, with lots of rocks bulging out of the walls and floor in irregular patterns. Molly peered nervously into the blackness. "I hope we're not too late," she murmured.

"Only one way to find out," Josh said. "Come on." Taking the flashlight from her, he stepped around the ladder and started down the tunnel.

Molly hurried up next to Josh. Luckily, the tunnel was wide enough for them to walk side by side. In silence they moved north.

Out of the dimness came a long, low sighing sound, like the heavy breathing of a giant.

Molly willed her heartbeat to slow down. "Wind, right?" she asked Josh.

He nodded.

They walked on. The hairs on the back of Molly's neck were prickling.

Suddenly the flashlight flickered. "Uh-oh," Josh muttered, shaking it.

The beam steadied. Molly swallowed her worry. "Let's walk faster" was all she said.

A couple of minutes later, Josh sniffed the air, then looked at Molly with a puzzled frown. "It smells different at this end," he remarked.

Molly breathed in deeply. Josh was right—the air did smell different here. The damp earthiness was stronger, and there was something else mixed in—a pleasant, roasted scent, sort of like spent matches.

She was the one who first figured it out. As they neared the island's northern end, Molly began to notice that there were piles of freshly fallen soil on the tunnel floor. Suddenly, she realized what the smoky smell was.

Dynamite.

"Josh," she said, trying not to sound too worried. "These piles of dirt are new. The tunnel has already begun to collapse from the blasting."

Josh's green eyes grew round as he took in what she was saying.

"We better not hang around here, O'Brien," he said. "I bet this whole area is pretty dangerous."

"We won't stay long," she promised. "But we can't let Mary McPhail down. We'll get out as soon as we find that book."

"Then let's start looking," Josh said.

He swung the flashlight in a slow arc from side to side. The two friends advanced cautiously through the tunnel.

A faint patter made them both jump. "Probably just a rat," Josh said after a minute.

Molly shook her head. "I almost wish it was," she said, pointing up to the ceiling. "But it's coming from up there. There's dirt falling down from the ceiling."

Josh stared at her. "Yikes!"

"Yeah," Molly agreed. She tried to sound calm, but there was a tight knot of worry in her stomach.

"O'Brien, look!" Josh said suddenly. He aimed the flashlight ahead of them.

It showed a mound of fresh debris as high as Molly's head, smack in the middle of the tunnel. To get around it they'd have to scramble over its sides. All around it, soil was sifting down from the ceiling in steady trickles.

Josh was already climbing over the dirt and rocks. Molly followed. Her feet sank into damp soil up to the ankles. "When we get back to the Hewitts', Grandpa's going to kill me for coming down here," she muttered. "And when we get home and my mom sees my new jeans, *she's* going to kill me, too."

"My mom's already at the Hewitts'. So at least I'll get it all at once," Josh said. "Any sign of that book?"

Molly gazed around. "No."

"It's ten to seven," Josh told her. "We should start back."

"After we came this far?" Molly cried. "We can't! Let's look for another five minutes. We'll run all the way back. I won't wimp out this time, I promise."

They walked along in silence for another minute or two, side by side with their heads down, staring at the tunnel floor. Suddenly Josh stumbled and gave a sharp exclamation of pain. "Ow! I banged my—"

As he broke off, Molly looked up. And then she felt a cold weight of hopelessness settle on her like a cloak.

The way ahead of them was completely blocked.

Giant boulders and other rubble lay in a heap up to the ceiling of the tunnel. There was absolutely no way they could get around it or through it.

They had failed.

Josh rubbed his ankle, which he'd banged on a projecting rock. "Let's go," he said gloomily. "There's nothing we can do."

Tears pricked Molly's eyelids. "Sorry, Mary," she whispered.

Turning, they began to trudge back the way they had come.

As they reached the smaller mound of debris, the flashlight flickered again, for a longer moment this time. Josh shook it, then threw a worried look at Molly. "I think it's going."

But Molly wasn't listening. Her ears had picked up the faintest of sounds off to the left. "Shh!" she commanded.

In the silence, she heard it again. *Plink. Plink.* "Did you hear that?" she asked Josh.

"Hear what?"

"That plinking." Molly pointed. "It was coming from over . . ."

She trailed off, her mouth opening in astonishment as Josh aimed the flashlight where she was pointing.

In the wall was a small round opening.

"Was that there before?" Josh asked in a hushed voice.

Molly felt a chill. "*I* didn't see it."

"Me neither," Josh said.

Slowly Molly stepped forward. "O'Brien, there's no time to explore another tunnel now!" Josh said urgently. "It's two minutes to seven. And this place could collapse any second!""

"I'll just stick my head in," Molly answered. "It won't take a second. Give me the light."

With an irritated sigh, Josh handed her the flashlight. Molly beamed it into the opening.

Inside was a tiny round chamber, about the size of the O'Briens' kitchen table. Water dripped from the rocky ceiling with a steady rhythm. That was the sound Molly had heard.

On the floor of the chamber lay a small black book.

Molly gasped. "Josh! It's here!"

"You're kidding!" Josh crowded up beside her and peered into the chamber.

Rumble!

"The tunnel! It's collapsing!" Josh yelled. "We've got to get out of this branch!"

"Quick!" Molly cried. Darting into the chamber, she grabbed the black book and thrust it into the waistband of her jeans. "Let's go!"

Scrambling over debris, the two friends dashed toward Founder's Green. Behind them, the tunnel rumbled and shook. A boulder crashed down from the ceiling, then another.

Molly stumbled and almost fell. "Josh!" she yelled.

"Hurry!" he shouted. Grabbing her hand, he dragged her forward. "We're almost there!"

Racing full tilt, they flung themselves out the mouth of the tunnel that led to Rocky Point. An instant later, rocks and dirt cascaded down behind them. In seconds, it was as if the tunnel had never been there.

White-faced and shivering, Molly and Josh stared at the piled debris for a shocked moment. Then, without a word, they turned and ran on.

Even when they left the rumbling behind, Molly and Josh kept running. They didn't stop until they came out into the main branch.

That was when the flashlight finally died. In an instant Molly and Josh were in pitch darkness.

"Don't panic," Josh said in a shaky voice.

"It's all right!" Molly panted. "All we have to do is go straight. Keep your hand on the wall to guide you. And hurry! We're late!"

Molly would never forget the last leg of that trek, stumbling through the dark as fast as she could go, her left hand always touching cold, damp earth, her right stretched out in front of her.

Finally her fingers jammed against metal. "The ladder!" she yelled. "Josh, we made it!"

Up she climbed. Josh was right behind her. Then they were wriggling through leaf-mold and out onto

Mr. Hewitt's moonlit lawn.

"I can't wait to hear their explanation for this," a stern male voice said.

"Neither can I," a woman's voice replied.

Josh and Molly both gulped and looked up.

Standing in a semi-circle in front of them were Mr. Hewitt, Elsa Hewitt, Grandpa Lloyd, and Mrs. Goldberg. Carrie and Gwen were behind them, looking apologetic.

"We tried to make them go away," Carrie said. "But they knew we were up to something."

"Well?" Josh's mother said. She folded her arms and stared at Josh. "We're waiting."

He winced. "It's kind of a long story."

"But it was worth it," Molly declared, feeling suddenly bold. She pulled the book out of her waistband. "In here is the solution to a hundred-year-old mystery, we think. We're about to find out who really killed Martin Ames. And then Mary McPhail's ghost can finally rest in peace!"

CHAPTER THIRTEEN

"Well," said Grandpa Lloyd. His blue eyes were bright with interest. "I'm not saying this gets you off the hook, but—what do you say we all go inside and take a look at this book?"

Mr. Hewitt nodded. "Supper can wait."

Molly shot Josh a triumphant look. As they all trooped into the big house, she explained what they knew so far and what they had guessed.

"See, we think the person who hired Ames might have killed him," she finished, stamping her mud-caked shoes on the mat by the front door. "McPhail said Ames told him he had been threatened."

"And we think Ames might have written down the name of whoever hired him in this book," Josh added.

"Well, let's see!" Gwen exclaimed impatiently. "Read it!"

Now that they had finally arrived at the moment of truth, Molly was too nervous to go on. What if the book didn't tell them what they needed to know? She didn't think she'd be able to stand it.

"Here," she said, handing the book to Grandpa Lloyd. "You told us the story. Now you finish it."

Nodding, Grandpa gently opened the brittle binding and paged through the book. Molly could see columns of figures and spidery old-fashioned script. There was absolute silence in the room.

Then Grandpa looked up. "Well, what do you know," he said softly.

"What? What?" everyone cried together.

"It's all here." Grandpa tapped the book with a finger. "The man who hired Ames was none other than Charles Whartley!"

"The mayor?" Molly breathed.

"Hey, isn't that the guy who built this house?" Carrie asked her grandfather. When he nodded, she gave a pleased smile. "I knew his name had a 'wart' in it."

"We did it! We did it!" Gwen yelled, dancing around in a circle. "Hooray!"

"It makes sense!" Josh said, his face lit up with excitement. "*That* must be why the mayor was so gung-ho about leading the raid on the tunnels. He wanted to make sure he got to Ames before Ames could tell anyone who he was working for."

Molly shivered. "That's so cold-blooded!"

"And that's why the mayor made them seal up the tunnel entrances," Josh went on. "If the customs agents or anyone had started poking around down there, they might have found the black book."

"Even if they didn't find the book," Mr. Hewitt pointed out, "they would have found that one of the tunnels led right to Whartley's house. That wouldn't have looked good for him at all."

"Well, my goodness," Mrs. Hewitt said. "Who'd have thought you children would figure all this out a hundred years later?"

Josh beamed. But Molly had just thought of something that sobered her.

"We can't prove any of this," she pointed out. "I mean, the fact that Mayor Whartley was the one who hired Ames isn't proof that he killed him."

"It's enough," Grandpa Lloyd told her in a sure voice. "It's certainly enough to clear John McPhail. The case against the mayor is at least as strong as the case against McPhail ever was."

"You think so?" Molly looked hopefully at her grandfather.

He nodded. "Tell you what. Tomorrow after school I'll take you kids to see the town justice. We'll lay the evidence in front of her. And if I know Julia Winterbottom, she'll agree it's enough to clear John McPhail's record."

Molly, Josh, and Gwen high-fived one another's palms. "All right!" Josh said.

"I wish I could go with you guys," Carrie said enviously. "Mom and I are catching the morning ferry, though."

"You're leaving?" Molly asked, abruptly coming down to earth. She looked hesitantly at old Mr. Hewitt.

"Yes, we're going home," Mrs. Hewitt said. She smiled at her father-in-law. "But don't worry. We'll be back for lots of visits!"

Later that night, Molly sat on her bed in her nightgown, with Martin Ames's black book in her lap. By the glow of her bedside lamp, she pored over the notes made in his precise bookkeeper's hand so many years ago.

The more she thought about it, the more she was sure that Grandpa's plan would work. And once McPhail's record was publicly, officially cleared, his daughter's spirit could finally go to its rest.

Suddenly she gave a giant yawn. It had been a long day, full of action and excitement. Now Molly was ready for sleep.

She stretched and stood up, looking around for her book. Finally she spotted it on top of her dresser. As she crossed the room to get it, she glanced idly in the dresser-top mirror.

She caught her breath. There in the shadows

behind her own familiar face was another figure. Its blond curls were pulled back from its temples in an old-fashioned hairstyle. It wore a high-collared white lace dress. And its big blue eyes were fixed on Molly's with a grateful look.

The image's lips parted. "Thank you," it mouthed silently.

Heart in her throat, Molly turned around.

There was no one there.

Molly stood stock-still for a moment. Then her own lips curved into a smile.

"You're welcome," she said aloud. "You're very welcome, Mary McPhail."

WELCOME INN

Secret in the Moonlight
0-8167-3427-5 $2.95

Ghost of a Chance
0-8167-3428-3 $2.95

The Skeleton Key
0-8167-3429-1 $2.95
Coming in December 1994

The Spell of the Black Stone
0-8167-3579-4 $2.95
Coming in January 1995

Available wherever you buy books.